One Golden Day

Charles D'Amico

Copyright © 2020 Charles D'Amico

All rights reserved, including the right to reproduce this book or any portions thereof in any form whatsoever. For information, address
Blue Handle Publishing, LLC
2607 Wolflin #963 Amarillo, TX 79109

First edition April 2020

Cover & Interior Design: Blue Handle Publishing, L.L.C. ISBN: 978-1-7347727-1-5

For all those who have stuck with me through this journey:

My loving, supportive wife;
My mother looking down on me;
And the literary inspiration, whom I wish to write one hundred books for, my sister.

One Golden Day

1

The Day We All Dream Of

Amarillo, Texas, is a town that seems like it's in the middle of nowhere, but it *feels* like you're in the middle of everywhere. It just depends on your perspective. If you grew up in a small town of two thousand, even twenty thousand, then it feels like the big city in the panhandle of West Texas. There is always the debate that Lubbock is the big city of the panhandle, but that's for a different day.

Today is about the greatest day of my life, filled with butterflies and joy all at the same time. To think that in my mid-twenties I've been lucky enough to find the woman of my dreams. You might be asking yourself why I would be taking out time to share a bit about myself on my wedding day? It's because what better time to take a moment to reflect on how I got here? The last ten years have been crazy—beginning with starting high school with my twin sister and going to college together (well, partially). The last three years especially have been life-altering. Let me introduce myself to you. My name is Travis Golden, twenty-seven years old, born at the same time as a twin sister who is twelve minutes older than me (she reminds me of this fact regularly).

We are not your typical twins and although we did many things together, we did not always do *everything* together. Because my twin is a sister and not a brother, we had a different relationship as twins growing up. We were extremely close but led different lives. Oftentimes as you grow up as a twin, you are so close that no one can understand your bond. It's hard to socialize with anyone other than your twin. Still, in our situation and with our upbringing, we had a different view of the world around us. For starters, we were both great at sports from an early age, but when we were ten years old my sister suffered a freak accident playing softball when she stepped in a hole in the outfield, breaking her ankle and leg in multiple places.

One Golden Day

The rehab and healing process took almost a year, and it took a toll on her. She never wanted to push it again in any sport. She was always timid, afraid to be aggressive. By the time we were in high school she had given up competitive sports altogether. She would only do yoga and running for fitness, but nothing competitive. On the other hand, I continued to carry the competitive torch from that day forward. She was my number one fan, pushing me, coaching me, and giving me details and feedback that no one else had the nerve to. She would find that one thing that would drive me nuts and keep pushing it.

As I'm getting ready, fighting back the urge to vomit after a night with my friends as well as nerves on this day, I see my mother making her way over to me.

"Mom, I know what you're thinking, but I don't want to hear it right now. If you…"

Before I can finish my sentence, she cuts me off and gives me a big hug and a kiss on the cheek and whispers, "I'm so proud of you, Travis. You have picked the most amazing bride; she is as beautiful inside as she is outside. Your grandmother is looking down on you with a big smile; you know that, don't you?"

One Golden Day

"Mom, if you keep this up, I'm going to start crying. I'm already going to be struggling most of the day, but this is going to push me over the edge."

My mom always knows how to pull my heartstrings. Well, let's be honest. Every mom knows how to do that. Even the worst moms out there have a way of pulling at us. My mother had my sister and me when she was very young—four months after she graduated high school. Luckily, she didn't show and was able to go to a local community college. That means that with a mother who is only eighteen years older than you, it is a different relationship you have with her as well as with your grandmother. When my mother's mom passed away I was only twenty-two, and my mother was only forty. It was young for both of us to lose someone so influential in our life. My grandmother passed away from Alzheimer's when she was only sixty-four years old; it had begun around her sixtieth birthday. She was doing okay, but after a brutal accident, she was never the same and took a turn for the worse.

"Travis, you look amazing in your tuxedo, and I love the haircut too. It's about time you finally got a haircut. I know you enjoyed growing your hair out and looking like a surfer for the past year and a half, but I'm so happy to have my clean-cut boy back."

"Mom, stop it. I'm glad I could make you and my bride happy with a simple haircut. Do you remember the first time I wanted to grow my hair out and I had to convince you and Dad to let me do it?"

"Oh my God, I almost forgot! You were so cute. It was the end of your eighth-grade year, and you were going into high school and wanted to change your look so you'd have a better chance with the girls." My mom started laughing, along with some of my groomsmen.

Right then my best man and best friend since college, Chris, looked up with a huge-ass grin on his face, which coincidentally, was the same look he'd given me the night I met my bride to be. Chris and I had been working as bartenders at a local bar in Amarillo when she walked in with her group of friends. We laughed because often when a group of friends, all female, came into the bar there would be three to four of them max, but this group numbered seven. I remember we couldn't figure out if it was one group. We kept giving them a hard time, like two single male bartenders should when a large group of cute girls walks in.

I remember Leighton specifically not just because I ended

up marrying her, but because of how we met. As I walked up and asked her friend what she would like to drink, she started to yell at me (she had pre-gamed a bit before coming to the bar). I remember it like it was yesterday.

"Hey bar dude, hey you, sir, Bro, come on man. I just want a drink." Don't get me wrong, she was cute, but damn was this girl drunk. She was already stumbling all over. She had to know that all she would get out of me was a coffee or water.

I started to make my way to her. "Miss, you need to slow down, right now…" That's when it happened; she leaned over and just started throwing up all over the bar and all over me. Everything that she had gotten into that small frame of hers made its way out the same way it had gone in.

I mean, it's a great way to make a first impression. The place I worked was called Hoots Pub, a great local bar for concerts and local country talent that comes through West Texas. And that night was no exception. We had a sold-out show so I had to run home, change, and get back to work. I didn't see her for the rest of the night, for obvious reasons. A week later, a cute girl that looked just like her, dressed to kill in tight, torn jeans, high heels, a cute red top, and a short jean jacket walked up to me with that big West Texas hair, snapping her gum.

One Golden Day

"Hey, I need to talk to you, hey...hey!" I was a little busy at the time and was pretty sure that she was the girl who had thrown up all over me the previous week. I wasn't about to head back over for a second helping of tequila chum.

"I'll be over there in one moment as soon as I'm done over here. Give me a minute." I know I snapped at her, but come on, she *had* thrown up on me.

"Hey, Buddy, I got all dressed up for you, to come apologize for throwing up all over you last week. The least you can do is get your ass over here and give me your full attention. I think I deserve that much—mainly because I know I look damn good right now." And I'll tell you what, she did. I can say that knowing now that she isn't a cocky person; she isn't stuck-up. I can tell you she was just trying to build herself up for the conversation we were about to have.

I will come back to that story at another time, but the moment she'd thrown up on me, Chris
shot me a look of, *Dude that hot chick just threw up on you*. It was the same look that he shot me now when my mom dropped that nugget on the room.

"Wait, what is this story? I need to hear this shit immediately, and we have plenty of time to kill."

One Golden Day

Right then my mom started in on the story of how I came to her and sat her down about how it was time for *me* to decide how my hair looked and which clothes I wore. I wanted to look good for girls and my friends, and my mother shouldn't be making my fashion choices anymore. I could only imagine what it was like for a mother to have her little boy finally come to her all grown-up, but still so young, telling her he was ready to make his own decisions. Little did my friends know that was the least important part of the story. As usual, my mom was about to do some teaching.

2

The Summer before Our Eighth-Grade Year

There we were, about to take our last placement test for STARR in the lovely state of Texas. My sister and I grew up in Amarillo, in the windy panhandle of West Texas. Our mother was born and raised in Santa Fe, New Mexico, but her family had moved to Amarillo for work when she was in high school, which is where she met our father. But back to the exciting part of the story: eighth-grade standardized tests, heck yeah!

"Travis, I can't wait to get this over with. I know I've been studying, but I'm so nervous."

Terra was funny that way when it came to tests. She always wanted to set the tone; she wanted to be the best in the city, the region, the state. Her competitive nature came out in school, whereas mine came out in sports.

"Terra, I love you, and not just because you're my sister, but you really need to get back into sports. Being ultra-competitive about STARR testing is a problem," I said jokingly, but I was also as serious as one could be with their twin sister.

Terra and I are twin siblings, born twelve minutes apart. As I said earlier, she's the older one of the two, but she's also a pain in the butt. She is driven, competitive, and crazy intelligent, which makes her a wrecking ball when it comes to standardized tests. I know it sounds crazy, but this girl tries to get a perfect score on all of these things, even on studies about how to take the test properly, not just on the information the tests contain.

"Travis, you didn't study, you don't care about these things. You know all you care about is making sure you can pass each class so that you can keep playing football and basketball. And let's not forget your life-changing decision. You need to tell Mom later today."

"Don't forget baseball and track, and as for school Terra, don't judge me. You know I've always had the same philosophy with school. It's not about sports, but about what I feel is good enough. Getting a *B* is good enough for me."

I was trying to gloss over her bringing up my big decision since I was trying to not make a huge deal out of it. But I felt the summer between eighth grade and high school was going to be big for me. I needed to make some changes and define who I wanted to be as I entered high school. She and I chattered away back and forth for about twenty minutes until the teacher walked in, the bell rang, and the sweat started to bead on the back of Terra's neck. I could feel her nerves like I always could. Even as kids, I could feel her getting nervous from across the room. I don't know if it's that sibling connection, a twin connection, or what, but now it's going to be bugging me.

"Class, you have known this day would be coming all year. We have been preparing you, testing you, reminding you, and trying to get you ready for this test. Some of you took it very seriously." She shot a look at Terra and smiled. "Others, not so much." She then looked directly at me over the top of her glasses, with a glare.

"You will have the rest of the period to finish your test; you can use your scratch paper and your calculator; that is it. When you are finished, you will bring your test and scratch paper, turn it in, and have a great summer. You may begin…NOW!"

After about twenty minutes, two of the biggest jokers of the class walked up, turned in their test, high fived the teacher, and said, "See you next week for summer school." I guess they figured why even take a shot at the test when they knew where they stood. That's got to be rough—to sit at the bottom of the class and know you just don't get it, and you struggle no matter how hard you try. I know I don't put forth a valiant effort all the time. I do care; I just don't get anxiety about not getting an A. As long as I understand most of it or get a general idea and I'm interested, then I'm good. That's the difference. Other things have grabbed my attention. I know I have to put forth an effort in life and to attain the things I want to do in life. I'm a realist.

Terra is another one altogether; she takes my competitive nature on the field and court to a whole other level. For me, winning is great when I'm competing, but so many different things are involved. I want to constantly improve my best, do my best to improve those around me, and to win. Most importantly, I can't stand losing. That's the biggest difference, from what I've read, between the greatest winners in sports history, like Jordan, Brady, and Montana. It's the hatred of losing, not the wanting to win. We all like to win, we all want to win, but how many truly hate losing with all our fiber? I can tell you, I do.

One Golden Day

When it comes to academics, Terra has a drive for knowledge and being judged against others. She has a level of anxiety that keeps her up at night reading and taking notes. If she doesn't graduate high school early, I'll be amazed. My parents have sat us down multiple times to lecture us on our competitiveness and have tried to get us to let up, but it's just been inside of us since birth. The funny part is neither of our parents are competitive. They're as hippy as one can be without being a hippy.

For example, I remember getting in trouble two months ago because I snuck out of the house to hang out with some friends late on a Friday. Instead of getting mad at me they sat me down, gave me a hug, and we talked it through. Hey, I'm not sitting here arguing parenting styles, I'm just telling you what my childhood was like: a lot more hugging than fighting. When you look at that, having two hyper-competitive kids, it makes you wonder, but I think it started with that injury Terra had. We used to push each other as kids in sports, always trying to one-up each other. When she couldn't play anymore, we found new ways to push and challenge each other. I'm not nearly as supportive as Terra is though. She puts in more effort than I ever had, and I tell her that.

One Golden Day

The test was brutal, as expected, at least for me, but the issues I had were a little different from the ones Terra had. She was struggling with the anxiety of not knowing a few answers. It was driving at her—trying to get a perfect score—whereas I was more hoping to pass and do well enough to have a good showing. When it came to academics, I wasn't concerned about making the starting lineup, merely being on the bench. Terra, on the other hand, was trying to win state and national level titles with every test and project. Knowing that my summer was free after a long test day, I was looking forward to a great workout and maybe a good run. I couldn't wait. This was going to be my summer, my year.

As expected, I was done before her, but that's because she had to check every answer, check her work, and make sure she didn't miss anything.

"Hey, Sis, you know you crushed it. You've put in the work; please don't let this ruin next week. Especially not the first week of summer break."

"I know, Bro, but it's hard. It's like you knowing you have a big match coming up. Even if I told you it was a scrimmage you'd still want to do well. It's our nature; we want to push it."

"I know, it just pains me to see you down and full of

anxiety, my Sis. I like you smiling and having a good time. Think you can at least try and fake it?"

She responded with a huge smile, laughing a little. "Yeah, Bro, I got you. I don't want to ruin the beginning of your summer plans, the summer you grow out your hair, change your look, and become a new man for high school." As she finished, she punched me in the shoulder—hard I might add.

"Ouch! Sis, you always know the perfect spot to hit me and get that knot started. Even when we were younger, you would always get me perfectly."

As far back as I can remember, she always would hit me just right, in my shoulder, which would give me that tight feeing. If I took her toy, she would slug me in the shoulder. If I didn't follow her rules in whatever make-believe game we had going on, she'd slug me in the shoulder. If she was bored and wanted to start a wrestling match, yup, you guessed it, she slugged me. She had to make up for that lack of athletics after her injury and decided to take it out on my shoulder, but hey, that's what siblings are for: to make you stronger.

"Let's get back to the big stuff though, Bro. Do you really think everything is going to change when we go to high school? I mean, it's the same kids—just different teachers and surroundings."

"I don't know. I do know that people always say high school can make or break you, whether it's school, popularity, or sports. Think of it, this will set up how and where we go to college and what the next steps are. Don't get me wrong, I want to be popular, I want to have fun, but I also know college is going to be way more fun. So I need to pick my spots."

"You've overthought this way too much, Travis."

"You of all people can't give me crap about overthinking anything. Remember last month when you couldn't decide on a pizza topping? I thought you were going to need to be committed and given some tranquilizers just to get you through the night."

"Ha, very funny. You know I can get anxiety when I have to make a decision. Sometimes the smaller ones get me worked up the most. I don't know why, they just do."

She wasn't always this way. The decision thing had just begun this year and I was trying to get her to calm down, to realize people don't care as much as she thinks they do. They are more focused on how she presents what she's saying than the words coming out. That's the key in middle school and high school. It's about presentation, it's about perception. Those things will define your reality. I just hope I can master them before I graduate and it's too late.

We finally made it home, but before I could get both feet in the door, I heard: "Mom, Travis has something he needs to tell you. It's very important; maybe we should call a family meeting." Luckily my Mom quickly realized I was a bit uncomfortable.

"Terra, stop giving Travis such a hard time. First of all, how were your tests? Are you satisfied with your efforts?" Yup, that's the way my parents talk.

"Mom, Terra is just a pain. Yes, I did pretty well; luckily nothing caught me by surprise. I guess I paid attention a little bit this year in class."

"Terra, what about you? I know you can get worked up over big tests like this. I'm sure you did great, you always did. But how are you doing?"

Terra and Mom left the room, went down the hall, and continued talking. Mom was trying to calm her down to get her to slow down, get her to relax, and try not to overanalyze stuff before she had the details. Me, on the other hand, I'm a growing boy, so I went into the kitchen to make me a Scooby-size snack, a monster-size sandwich. It was awesome and had everything on it: three kinds of meat, two different cheeses, a crap ton of mayo and mustard, and a pile of dill pickles slopped together with the mayo and mustard. It was so good. It took a good thirty minutes to make it and clean up. I was just sitting down when Mom had come back and started giving me the biz.

"Travis, so what's this big news that Terra was giving you crap about? Do you have a girlfriend for the summer?" she said with that soothing "Mom voice" as she sat down at the kitchen table with me. I remember this day vividly because all day, Terra and my mom had been giving me crap about the big news. I just wanted to get through the next couple of days and enjoy the summer, but my sister was doing her best to play the role of an annoying sibling. That role is often reserved for me, but this time she took the reservation and ran with it, leaving me sitting in the waiting room to be heckled.

"Mom, I don't want to get into it right now, and no, I don't have a girlfriend. Is Terra finally calming down, or are we going to have to endure her moping around for the next couple days until she gets her test scores?"

"You know how your sister is. Just like you take sports seriously and put in the extra work, which can lead to anxiety and stress on game days, she gets worked up over tests.

Especially big ones like this. She knows they get ranked in the state, and she's trying to always stand out. You know she misses playing sports, but can't get over that hump."

"I know. I just don't want to look forward to the next couple of years starting off every summer with a sister moping around."

"I think she'll be fine. Just give her a few days to vent. Back to your big news. What's going on? Is there anything we can be excited about, or worried about?"

"Mom, it's nothing like that at all. Terra is just giving me a hard time; just leave it alone for now."

And on that note, I got up and started to walk out of the room as my mother was giving me shit about something. I couldn't tell because I had already started to put my headphones in and started listening to some music. I was going to get changed and go for a run, clear my head, and get ready for summer. As I was getting dressed about to head out, Terra stuck her head into my room, then plopped on my bed, just looking at me. She wouldn't say anything. She just stared at me, waiting for a response or a question. (She tends to do that when she's looking for a distraction.)

"You know, Sis, one thing always bothered me about those

tests. If smart people keep saying they are worthless why do we keep taking them, and why do you keep getting worked up over them?" I was doing my best trying to be a good brother. I can do that occasionally.

"You know, Travis, I don't know, but as long as they keep track of the scores and rank the top test scores in the state, I'm going to work my ass off to stand out. I can only imagine what it will look like on a college application if I'm one of the top scoring students every year. "

She had a point. It's how I would look at my mile times when running track, or scoring records when playing basketball. I love basketball: the sound of the ball hitting an empty court, the sound of the net, and the sound of the ball slapping hands on a perfect swish. There are so many things that bring me pure joy when I play basketball. It's not just that it brings out the competitive nature in me, there's something about it—whether it's making a great play to give a teammate a wide-open lay up or locking down the other team's best player and getting in his head. But I'd say my favorite part is a quiet day on the court, by myself, working through the stress of the week and improving my game a little bit at a time.

I remember reading a story about Jay Williams, former

One Golden Day

NBA player and current ESPN analyst about him practicing in the Staples Center the morning before a game. He was on one side of the net and Kobe Bryant was on the other. Jay kept working out, pushing himself harder than ever, dripping sweat. When he finished, Kobe practiced for another hour or two. A year or so later Jay Williams was out of the league due to injury.

He asked Kobe about that. He said he would never let a player outwork him, especially in his house. That's the drive I have when I practice. When I compete, I'm going to put the work in, outwork my opponent, and not let them feel or see me weak. "Terra, I get it. When it comes to competitions you and I only have one speed. You know one day it might catch up to us, but I feel like because we have each other, we can keep pushing each other to great things."

"Bro, I love you. Thank you for getting me and understanding why I'm so nuts."

"Shit, Sis, I don't get it, but I accept it and support you being crazy just like me."

Then we gave each other a big-ass hug and I finished getting ready and went out for a long run, then came home and started shooting hoops. It's where I do my best thinking. I know. A kid not even in high school worried about things like that, but you have to build a routine if you're going to be successful and you're never too young to start.

After a good hour of shooting and sweating, Mom came out and started in on me again.

"Travis, you shoot, I'll rebound, not to mention you need to work on going to your left. And when you do, your shot is a mess, so you'll need lots of rebounds."

"Mom, you're funny. I guess I can put up with you out here. But better not be trying to pry any information out of me; you know I don't want to talk about it."

Before I knew it, my mom was getting me to talk to her as though I was lying on the couch in her psychotherapy office. She was always good at finding the right time, the right way, and the right words to get your darkest secrets out. I get it. Perhaps mine was not quite a dark secret, but it was still important to me. It's something I'm a little embarrassed about and that I don't want to talk about. But when your mom is out on the driveway throwing you passes, rebounding bad shots, and pushing you, you'll tell her anything.

"So, this is going to be a big summer for you, going to high school next year. I know you want a chance at being a freshman on varsity. Are you ready to work this summer?"

"Mom, you know I am. You know I'm already putting in the work, and you know that's not what this is about. I'm almost certain Terra already told you what the big news is. I'm going to grow out my hair and really work on my look this summer. I know it may seem shallow, but high school is important, and I don't want to make any mistakes."

We spent the rest of the night, and many other summer nights, out on that driveway shooting hoops. When she wasn't helping my sister study, get ahead, and talk about books they were reading, she was pushing me, keeping up with me on the court. Each pass felt like a day of summer. I could feel the sweat on my palms from the moment I woke in the morning until the first time I shot for the day. I think over the summer I easily shot three to five hundred times a day, every day, for the summer.

Over that summer, my mother and I spent hours talking about everything from girls to family to friends and school. She found a way to tutor me, to prepare me for my freshman year while I was shooting, dribbling, and sweating. I can still hear her in my ear, pushing me, coaching me, being my biggest supporter. She may not have been aggressive, competitive, or

One Golden Day

a driving force, but she was the ultimate coach.

"Let me get this straight, Mrs. Golden. His big plan going into high school was to grow out his hair and change his clothes? He had to know that being a jock, and a great one at that, would carry him further. Why do I feel like you went Mrs. Golden on us and changed that story trying to give us some wisdom halfway through that story?" Chris was excited.

"You know she did. You guys have been around her long enough to know that my mom can tell a tale and get you sucked in."

"I don't know whether to be flattered or insulted by my own son on his wedding day."

"Mom, you know we love you, just sometimes you have a tendency to give a sermon. This time it so happened to be in the back of a church."

My mom always found a way to grab an audience. She was amazing like that. Terra was the same way. She could always command a room. She just didn't realize it as much as my mother did. Then again, Mom had some more life experience under her belt.

"Mom, do you have a few minutes? Maybe we could go for a walk out back one last time before the big event."

27

One Golden Day

"I did see a hoop out there. But I don't know if anyone has a ball for you to calm your nerves." "It's not that, Mom. I just want to talk; to take a few moments to be quiet.

One Golden Day

3

Amazing How Much You Can Miss Someone

It's been too long since she passed away, and I'll never forget the way she would smile at me. My grandma had a massive impact on my life. My mom worked a lot growing up and put time in with us at school, which meant one of us was left without. If Mom was with Terra working on a school project or on a field trip, however, I could always count on Grandma to be there when I got home. She was the constant in our lives; the thing we knew we could always count on. No matter the weather, Grandma was always there. That's what made it so hard when she was diagnosed with Alzheimer's because it was more than just losing her. It was losing her mind, her ability to be the rock we'd all grown up with.

"Travis, do you want me to look for a ball, to help you calm down? The hoop looks rough, but I think you could still find a rhythm."

"You know I can find a rhythm on any rim, Mom. It doesn't matter. We worked on so many shots over the years, it doesn't matter, just give me a few shots to find the range and I'm automatic," I said with a joking smile on my face.

"You know your grandma loved watching you play. We all did. The joy you got when you won, how hard you were on yourself when you lost—you always made us so proud."

Having my grandmother there always gave me a sense of comfort, like a security blanket. No matter how bad I was playing or feeling, I would look to her in the stands and see her calmness, and it would just level me out. She had a way about her that lacked judgment with her grandkids. I know her relationship with my mother wasn't the same as it was with us, but what grandparent isn't a bit different with their kids than they are their grandkids?

"Thanks, Mom, I just wish she could have been here. I know how much she loved Leighton. She knew after only a few months of dating we would end up together. She used to tell me 'Don't let this one go, she's special.'"

"Your grandma always had that gift, you have it too. She could read people and see their true selves quickly. But the

One Golden Day

biggest thing was her ability to step up for you and Terra; she would jump in no matter the situation."

"Yeah, that's true. I remember that time our basketball coach got the flu during our basketball tournament game and couldn't finish coaching. She stepped up when no one else wanted to. Well, with Terra's help she did."

"Your grandma loved that story. She would rarely tell it, but she would light up when she heard you or Terra tell it."

I'm referring to a summer basketball tournament before my eighth-grade year, and our coach had gotten brutally sick. It was about five minutes into the game. He kept running to the bathroom, and I remember my grandma kept asking him if he was going to be okay. He looked at her with the fear of God in his eyes, probably afraid he was going to throw up all over the court. He took off running, and we kept playing. At the next clock stoppage the ref looked to our bench and asked the team where our coach was and said if we didn't have a coach by the next time-out we would have to forfeit. That's when Grandma stepped up and started barking at the ref. The ref told her to either take over coaching or shut up. So she stepped up and started coaching.

"Grandma, do you even know what you're doing?" I looked at

One Golden Day

her, puzzled.

"No idea, but I have Terra and you. She knows just as much as you and she can help me while you're out on the court."

"Wait a minute. I'm going to do *what*? All of a sudden, I'm now sucked into being Grandma's assistant coach for your game?" I addressed Terra who looked intrigued and pissed at the same time. She always loved a crazy challenge.

"Come on, Terra, you know you like winning just as much as your brother does, and you can probably do just as well or better than their coach. You always tell me in the stands that he doesn't know what he's doing." Grandma had a point; Terra, even in the seventh grade was smarter than most youth coaches. She had a knack for sports and understanding them. She just feared them after she'd had her accident.

"Alright. I'm in if Terra's in. I'm not about to lose this game because our coach can't keep from throwing up."

"That's the spirit you two! What about the rest of you? Are you guys game to get coached by an old lady and her thirteen-year-old granddaughter?" As she eyeballed the whole team they all said, "Yes," loud and proud.

The game started off a little rocky, as would be expected. We had some work to do and I got

One Golden Day

a little carried away trying to show off for the other kids and my grandma. Terra had Grandma call a time-out, pulled me off the court, and told me to start passing like crazy to calm my nerves. If the ball came back to me, then look to make a play. All of a sudden, I started getting into a rhythm and so did the team. However, we still were trading baskets more than anything, and we were at risk of bowing out of the tournament much earlier than I would have liked.

At halftime, we sat there and I sulked a bit because the high and excitement had worn off and I was getting inside my head. Terra started doing her best Mickey and Rocky routine, getting me to pull my shit together and get back on the horse.

"Travis, what are you doing out there? You are you a bum, you look like a bum. Your missing layups, missing jumpers, and you're not even passing to the open man. Hell, you're not even guarding your guy, you're acting like a Spanish bullfighter, and doing that..." I cut her off before she got too riled up.

"Terra, I got it. I need to relax and just play, and you were right earlier when I started passing first. I need to let the game come to me."

Then Grandma chimed in, making sure I was getting a

licking. "Terra, are you giving Travis the business over there? Make sure he knows he's about to lose this game if he doesn't quit acting like a selfish idiot. His team needs him to keep them involved."

"I'm already on it, Grandma."

You might be asking yourself why it is so important to me on my wedding day to be bringing up this moment in my life. The women in my life have played a huge role in the man I am today: my mother always showed me what it means to sacrifice, push, and still do your best to be there for your family. My grandmother always showed up no matter what the situation, until she needed us to carry the load. Then there was my sister Terra, the rock in my life, the person who always pushed me to be better, day in and day out.

But this day was huge for me, especially as an athlete, but more importantly as a person. I learned about teamwork that day on the court, about stepping up when you're needed most, and learning to share the limelight. My grandmother was the one who stepped up. My sister really saved the day and kept us together, and I was ruining all of it with poor game-play.

Once my sister and grandma got into me and pushed me to be a better teammate and let the game come to me instead of forcing it, we came back and won. The important part wasn't simply the winning part, but the way we did it. I only scored eight points in the second half, but I assisted on fifteen baskets and had twelve rebounds to go with it. My final line for the game was nineteen points, twenty assists, and sixteen rebounds. I learned that I could impact the game and my team and stand out without being the ball hog I thought I needed to be.

Terra pushed me that day, every day, but we really bonded over basketball. I grew to trust her as an adult, more so than any of my coaches, because I knew she would always be honest with me. Grandma too showed me she would always be there and would always stand up for me and even coach if she had to. She did this to ensure that I was going to be given every opportunity to win or lose on my own merit. She rode me harder than anyone but I know she did it out of love, and I cherished it. She had a way about her. She could tell you something with a smile that would cut you at your core. I remember that after the game she made a comment to one of our guards about his shot.

"Great job, guys. Way to fight and come back and win. Steve, way to keep shooting out there. I can see you've been working hard on that shot even if none of them went in."

As I said, she could say it with a smile, say it sweet, and still cut you down. Luckily Steve also struggled with paying attention and was too busy looking around the gym and missed most of what Grandma had said. After the game was over, the coach finally made his way out of the bathroom only to tell us he was sorry and that he was going to an urgent care and he would get a hold of Coach Grandma before day's end to see if he needed her to coach again the next day.

"Terra, thank you for pushing me at halftime. I needed that. We needed that, as a team. You always know how to get to me."

"Travis, I would hope so. We are twins, ya know. We are identical in almost every single way, and we're wired the same way. I just told you what I would have needed to hear. I'm glad you listened; it feels just as good on this end watching someone lead their team with the direction you gave them."

Terra could do anything she put her mind to. She could master a skill, learn a new subject, fix a problem, or solve a riddle. It might take her time, but she wouldn't quit until she figured it out. For me, it's that way with a skill or a trait I'm trying to master for basketball especially, and football a bit.

One Golden Day

That day was spent sharing the win with my team. We were so excited to go from potentially forfeiting the game, being lucky enough to play it, and then winning it. For me it was about growth as a teammate, a player, and a brother; learning to trust, learning to be a leader, and sharing the spotlight—and to understand that there is plenty to go around.

The car ride home took a while, but we spent most of the time talking and laughing, making the ride feel like it was only five minutes long.

"Grandma, I just really wanted to say thank you for stepping up like that, it was amazing. You didn't need to do that."

"Yes, I did Travis. I didn't see anyone else stepping up to the plate to help out, and anyone who would have might have lacked the will to ask Terra to lead the way. She was our secret weapon today. She kept you guys in the game and made sure you stayed on point."

Grandma, as usual, was "on point."

"I think she's fallen asleep in the back from all the excitement. Yup she's out, which makes me a bit surprised that I'm not asleep myself. Today was a rollercoaster and one heck of a game."

One Golden Day

"Travis, you played your heart out. I've never been so proud of you. You started off poorly, only to work your way—and your team—back into the game, doing the hard stuff that needed to be done, not the pretty stuff. I hope you learn that this is how life is going to be. You're going to have days where you need to focus on hard work, let others shine, and enjoy the fruits of your teamwork. If you are always looking to be out front, you will leave too many people behind and miss the true joy that comes from working together." Grandma had a big smile on her face as she was talking to me.

"I know, Grandma. I learned a lot from today. I promise I won't let you down after today."

I didn't, don't get me wrong. There were growing pains and as there are with any person growing up, I had my good days and my bad months. But I always came back to what I learned that day, often because Terra or Grandma wouldn't let me forget it. They would hammer it into my head telling me, "Don't forget about the Parma Tournament; don't forget it takes a team." That summer and that game has stuck with me and reminded me of the man I want to become, the man I am now, and the man I choose to be.

One Golden Day

Before I realized it, Mom had found a ball. She probably had one in the car the whole time. Soon enough we were shooting hoops out back of the church, talking about Grandma and how much we missed her.

"Mom, I know you said that you and Grandma didn't always see eye to eye or get along. But you knew she was trying to make up for your childhood by helping us as much as she did. Do you still feel that way years later?" I hoped that, to my Mom, I didn't come off as crass.

"No, Travis. I sometimes do, but after raising you and your sister and dealing with everything we've dealt with over the years, I realize we all do the best with what we've got. We can't judge
people; we can only have empathy when we don't understand or agree with their choices or decisions. Getting angry won't make it any better or solve it. Your grandmother went above and beyond to help you and Terra, and I'm forever grateful for that. I know she never had that same help."

"You said Mom and Grandpa met before he went off to war. That's when she got pregnant with you, and they got married quickly trying to hide the pregnancy. But her parents got mad and pretty much disowned her?"

One Golden Day

"That's the general idea of it. Back then, times were different. Families were embarrassed or ashamed if their kids did something like that. They'd rather disown them then own the poor choice. I know it seems really odd now, looking back, but times have changed."

Mom wasn't kidding.

My daughter, my life, and my family would be different if I'd been born when Grandma was.

One Golden Day

4

Family Vacation Turned Political Incident

Mom and I were still out there shooting hoops when my best friend and best man, Chris, stuck his head out back, screaming at us. I couldn't make out anything he was saying, so I screamed back, which wasn't the brightest idea, 'cause chances were he wouldn't hear me either.

"I can't hear you, Chris, come out here." I guess it worked, or he gave up since he quickly ran over.

"I couldn't hear you. What did you say, and what are you guys doing out here?"

"What's it looks like? We're shooting hoops and talking; you've known me long enough to know that's a constant." Chris has been on the other end of this basketball.

"Well, I might as well get some shots in too, kill some time. Got any great stories, Mrs. Golden?"

"Actually Chris, Travis and I were talking about his

grandma and sister. He has a story that I'm not sure he's ever told you because it's kind of a family secret. But under the circumstances, I think he can tell it."

"Mom, really, you think that's a good idea?" It was a great story about my grandma and Terra almost starting an international incident.

"Travis, now you *have* to tell it. If you're reluctant, your mom is telling you it's okay. Do I need popcorn for this?" Chris asked. He can sometimes act like an eager golden retriever puppy, but his pure joy and excitement for life is one of his best qualities.

"Alright, I'll tell the story, but this stays between us. You got it, Chris?" I gave him that look two guys give each other when they are trying to tell the other one to lock it up; nothing gets said. "Travis, I got it, Bro. You know I'm not going to tell your sister, or anyone else for that matter."

The story goes something like this: for Christmas break our freshman year of college, our parents surprised us and took us on a trip to Washington, D.C. It was a huge deal for my sister because it was a dream of hers to attend Georgetown University and get into politics. The summer before our freshman year of college, she got a job interning at the mayor's

One Golden Day

office in Amarillo and, through hard work and persistence, or sisterly nagging, was able to get a piece of legislation passed on the local level and moved to be heard at the state level. It was a big deal, not just for her, but for the city. It made the papers and gave the city and mayor some clout on

the state stage, allowing them to make a push for a senate race coming up. They were going to work with Terra on this, given the fact that she had put so much work into getting the bill passed in Amarillo.

Terra worked with the city council to incentivize helping the homeless utilizing apartment complexes with vacancies, motel rooms, or houses that already had a room-share situation in place. In these cases, the owner of the residential unit, utilizing their spaces to get someone off the street for a minimum of ninety days, could receive a tax rebate on their property taxes. This helped pull people off the street, which helped the city budgets, butalso improved living conditions for many. The way Terra looked at it was that so many people were already helping those in need they should get something for it. If they got some help, it might allowthem to help even more people and encourage others to do the same.

Because of this attention, she was offered a chance to tour

the office of senator for District 31, which is where Amarillo is. Mom and Dad wanted to reward her by taking us on a cool trip and found that the week starting on New Year's was a good time to line it up. We all went out as a family and took Grandma with us. I should preface this by saying this was right around the time that Grandma's mind started slipping. She wasn't completely disconnected yet, but she was starting to have just as many off days as good days. My mom didn't want to leave her home, given that the rest of us would be gone for a week. So we decided it would be one last trip with Grandma, and we would all keep an eye on her. You can only imagine how this is going to end up: an ornery old lady who's also losing her mind making her way around D.C. when it's at half capacity from the holidays. This is what authors call "foreshadowing of something bad to come," or "hilarious." It just depends on your point of view.

It was January fourth, and we'd been in town a day and a half and had done some of the basic touristy stuff, like the Lincoln Memorial and the entire National Mall. You really can't fathom the size of the Lincoln statue until you're standing there and realize how insignificant you feel. We went around the Smithsonian, looking at all the artifacts from various periods of history. Dad loved the TV stuff, like the signpost from the TV show *M.A.S.H.* in the National Museum of American History. I honestly enjoyed the entire trip. It was a cool city and I loved the overall historic part; the architecture was cool. The way they designed the city so you could see the capitol building from anywhere, with no buildings higher than it, was just awesome. Then there's the historic town of Alexandria, Virginia, right next to D.C.

The roads and walkways that have been barely touched since the time of Washington gives you that draw on history, that tactile feel.

Now back to Grandma and the international episode she and Terra caused. It started with a scheduled tour with our representative John Cornyn, who had been in office since 2002 and was born and raised in the Houston, Texas, area. His office staff was gracious and amazing. He, on the other hand, was quickly enamored with my grandmother. However, he didn't realize her condition, nor did we mention it. At the time, we were still having trouble dealing with it ourselves.

My grandmother stood about five feet five inches tall when she wasn't wearing heels, which she often did. She was always dressed to impress, as a good West Texas lady should be, which

One Golden Day

is what she would tell Terra and my mother quite regularly. On this day, because she knew we were going to see a senator, she was dressed to impress, wearing her favorite little black dress, heels, and a small jacket, and probably freezing. I just remember watching the senator's eyes gravitate to her the moment she walked into the room. I'm not saying he was rude or a dog, but any man seeing a beautiful woman his own age is oftentimes engaged in conversation quickly.

"Hello, you guys must be the Golden family. Are you Mr. and Mrs. Golden with Travis and obviously Terra? But who is this ray of sunshine with you?" With that, he grabbed my grandmother's hand, escorting her to the front of the group.

"I am Terra's grandmother, but you can call me Mimi. It's a pleasure meeting you. I've never met a senator before. Your office is beautiful." Grandma, like the rest of us, were quite awed.

"Well, Mimi, thank you for coming with your family, and Terra, thank you for all the work you did back in Amarillo. It takes people like you to make big changes in the world. It takes small changes in our communities before we can big changes at our state and federal levels."

"Thank you, senator. I really appreciate the opportunity

One Golden Day

to come out to D.C. and meet with you and see D.C. up close. I'm grateful for the invitation and the time you've taken to see us." Terra was almost blushing.

"I'm simply doing what is right, thanking a great person from our state, and your parents are the ones to be thanked here. They raised you and got you out here. Thanks again, Mr. and Mrs. Golden, for coming here this week. What have you seen so far? Have you been to the Library of Congress yet?"

My mother answered quickly, "No, we haven't, we have only done the National Mall and Smithsonian so far and a little bit of Alexandria. We were hoping to get in there today, but saw it was closed."

"Yes, they are doing some maintenance all week, but I bet you we can get you in there and past the normal security restrictions, especially since the building is closed up. I've got an idea; how about my office orders us some sandwiches for lunch? We can talk, get to know each other, then we can head over once we get it all cleared."

"That would be amazing, senator. You are too kind, thank you so much. We are already grateful for your time; this would be a once in a lifetime opportunity." My mother was getting a little hyper as she was shaking his hand.

One Golden Day

"Yes, senator, thank you so much, we are forever grateful for your kindness," Terra chimed in, trying to get Mom to calm down.

After an hour of lunch and talking with the senator and his staff, you could see Terra was hooked, ready to be a politician or at least work in politics. She's always had an eye for change, having been dialed in locally in Amarillo, but this was different. Here she was getting to see what it was like at the big leagues; getting that taste. One of the senator's top aides was a female who had stepped off to the side with Terra and spent most of the time talking with her. As expected, the senator had spent most of his time talking with my parents and my grandmother.

We made our way over to the Library of Congress, which was a short walk though a cold one in January. It wasn't too bad. It was almost forty degrees out and sunny, which made it feel pretty good. It's not much warmer in Amarillo this time of year, but the lack of moisture in West Texas keeps the feeling of cold to a minimum. You don't realize it until you're in a climate that has that cold air mixed with moisture that just sits on your skin and chills you to your core. I don't know how my grandma did it—walking around in those heels and that dress—but she

One Golden Day

didn't waiver once.

"We're almost there. Once we get inside, I'll have to go talk to a few colleagues, but my staff will be able to help you get around. We'll have an hour inside. They said the staff is off for the rest of the day."

My grandma made sure to flirt with the senator a few more times before he had to exit stage right. We never did see him again. That was a pretty good exit strategy: getting us into the Library of Congress when it was closed, giving us access we wouldn't otherwise get, and then dipping out the side door. His staff was great, but they slowly started disappearing one at a time until we were left with two people who seemed to be interns—or at least the lowest people on the totem pole. At this point, we were walking around the main areas that the general tour allows. This encompassed the stairs, the hallways, and the library itself, but not where the books are. The ceilings, walls, and detail were beautiful and made you feel like you were walking in a painting. I could imagine someone who had to take a weeklong trip across the frontier to get to D.C., and then see that building, those walls, and the ceiling. They must have been absolutely mesmerized.

"Hey, Mom, where is everyone? I only see, well, you and

One Golden Day

me." I looked at Mom, perplexed.

"Your dad had to go; he went back to the hotel when we made our way over here. He had some work to do; you didn't realize that?" Obviously that was the case, otherwise, I wouldn't have asked.

"No, but that doesn't explain where Terra and Grandma went, not to mention where are our chaperones? The bottom lackeys left after all the important people left." Judging by the look my Mom gave, she didn't like the way I'd described them.

"First of all, don't call them lackeys. Second, I have no idea where any of them are. Let's go look."

She grabbed my hand and we went hunting around the library. It took us a good twenty minutes of searching before we realized there was no one in the building but us. However, we still hadn't found Terra or Grandma, which started to get us worried. They also weren't answering their cell phones. Then when we were upstairs in the hallway, I could hear Terra's cell phone going off, but it was coming from the library itself. I kept hearing it but still didn't see her, however, eventually I could. The only problem was that she and Grandma had handcuffs on and were sitting down against the wall. In the library with security Terra looked pissed and

One Golden Day

Grandma looked lost.

"Mom, I found them, but you're not going to be too happy." I turned to grab her and pull her over to me.

"Travis, spit it out. Where are they?" she said with a panic in her voice.

"Terra and Grandma are down in the library, and from the looks of it they are getting arrested."

"What! We need to get down there."

The problem was that there was not an easy way to do that, at least not one we knew of. And I had no quick way to get anyone's attention, so I tried to think quickly on my feet. I grabbed my phone and started calling Terra again. I also started screaming to get her and the officer's attention, and finally got them to answer her phone.

"Officer? I'm going to give my phone to my mother, who is also the mother of the young woman you have down there. Is that okay?"

"Sure, I'll have the other officer come grab you guys so we can figure out what's going on."

"Officer, why are my daughter and my mother handcuffed and sitting on the floor of the Library of Congress?" You could tell my mom was doing everything she could to not lose it.

One Golden Day

"Ma'am, wait for the officer to come grab you. We'll talk in person and try to get this squared away."

We waited for what felt like an hour but was more like five minutes. The officer, or security guard, I'm still not sure to this day who he worked for, came and grabbed us and escorted us. There was an awkward silence that could only parallel having your parents drive you on a date when you were in your twenties. We made our way down to a back corridor, down a winding set of steps and a back hallway, where he opened the door to the library itself. The smell of old leather, cleanliness, and history just hit me. I could only imagine what Terra had felt when she walked in there; it would be like walking into Madison Square Garden to shoot a free throw for me.

"Terra, Grandma, are you two okay? What is going on? Why are you two in handcuffs? And how did you two get in here? Officer?" My mom was starting to lose her cool a bit about this point.

"Mom, we're okay, Grandma is in and out a bit. She knows who she is, but she thinks I'm a friend of yours, not your daughter. That's kind of how we ended up here in the first place. I'm sorry about this," Terra said.

"Ma'am, that's what we're trying to figure out. I have

another officer reviewing the security footage as we speak, as well as confirming her story with the senator about how you and your family got in here in the first place, with it being closed all week. If all checks out, you guys will be on your way. I apologize for the handcuffs, but there are a lot of security issues involved with this room."

"Do we have any idea how long this might take? I need to call my husband and let him know what's going on. Travis, can you…"

"Mom, I started texting him the moment you got off the phone with the officer a few minutes ago. He's already on his way; he'll message when he's outside." I'm impatient, I know. "Thanks, Travis, you've always been good with that stuff. Terra, are you and Grandma okay?
And you really don't remember how you got in here?"

"Mom, I was so worried about Grandma I wasn't paying attention to anything else, I just wanted to make sure she was okay. I was chasing her down, trying to get her to pay attention and
stop moving away from me. She was frantic and talking in circles. I have never seen her this bad."

Terra gave my mother the look of all looks, trying to get her to understand how bad Grandma really was, but I don't think my mother was figuring it out very well because she was trying to talk to her as if nothing had happened, which drove Terra up the wall. The only thing keeping Terra from grabbing Mom and pulling her to the side to give Mom an earful was those handcuffs and the officers.

"Mom, why did you run away from Terra like that, you know better, especially since we were guests of such a nice senator, who you were flirting with." She was talking to my mother like nothing had happened. I finally pulled her aside because I saw what Terra was trying to get Mom to notice about Grandma.

"Mom, I don't think you're grasping what Terra is trying to tell you. Do you realize what happened here? Grandma's slipping, she's slipping badly. She doesn't know who Terra is, she doesn't know who you are—that's what's going on." I was rough but then again, I have always been a little blunt in situations like this. That's how Terra and I have always been.

"Travis, you watch your mouth when you're talking to me. As for you, Terra was it, is it..." All of a sudden, it all started getting to Mom.

"Yes, Mom, it was and is that bad. I don't know if or when

One Golden Day

she's going to snap back; this is the worst I've ever seen it."

You could see it in Terra's face. She looked lost, distraught. There was just a level of uncertainty I hadn't seen since her injury as a kid. Eventually, my dad got into the building and joined us. I'm not sure how, but then again, the next hour was kind of a blur. There was a lot of arguing, debating, or loud conversing about someone in the room. After about fifteen minutes, the security officer took the handcuffs off of my grandmother and sister but wouldn't let us leave until they got some more clarification on what had happened. We had to wait around until the main aid for the senator came over with a signed letter from the senator confirming the story. He also took responsibility for his staff, for he had left a group of unauthorized civilians in the Library of Congress without supervision.

It really was a big deal, but the security guard was trying to downplay it and keep it under wraps, however, the senator and his staff had really messed up. Well, his staff had really messed up, not so much the senator; he trusted his key people to handle a simple tour for a family from the Texas panhandle. But little did they know we had an ace up our sleeve: the international criminal

One Golden Day

known as Mimi. She was dressed to the nines, ready to roll. She had a secret weapon—plausible deniability—no matter what, because her memory was going. I know it's not nice to joke about, but when you deal with it day in and day out, laughter is the only way you can survive the roughest of days.

At one point, my grandmother spent a good twenty minutes arguing with the officer. She was trying to take her handcuffs off because she wasn't even sure why they were on in the first place. She struggled to recognize her own daughter, our mom, and was more convinced that Terra was her daughter. We just had to go with it in order to get Grandma calmed down and under control. Terra rolled with it and got Grandma to focus and follow suit. She eventually got her off to the side while Mom and Dad and I tried to square this mess with the security officers (I say to myself, like I had done anything other than texting Dad to get up there).

"Okay, Golden family, it looks like everything checks out, but we are still waiting on some formality items to be cleared before we can let you go. It should be much longer; I know you didn't expect to be sitting in the Library of Congress all day. I do appreciate your patience, but you can understand that with the circumstances we have to be careful."

He had a point, for two people had been found walking around a closed-off part of the library without credentials. One seemed to be playing dumb or senile, and the other was young and intelligent. It didn't look good. It turned out Grandma saw a security guard walk through a doorway. She caught the door before it closed and made her way into the hallway before it closed. Terra followed suit, trying to keep tabs on her. Before they knew it, when trying to find a way out, they were in the library, a place they were not supposed to be.

I finished telling Chris the story. By this time, he had stopped dribbling and held the basketball in his hands. "Wait a minute, so let me get this straight, Travis. You're telling me that back when you were a freshman in college, your sister and grandma accidentally broke into the Library of Congress in Washington, D.C.? In doing so, they probably got a senator's staff in some deep shit, too? This is amazing. Why have you never told me this?" Chris had a huge smile on his face and was dribbling the ball again.

"It's a family story. It's not like this is something I can just bring up casually in a conversation. And if you're going to sit over there with the ball, put it to use and either pass it to me to shoot, or start shooting yourself. It's my wedding day, after all." I looked at my mother for some confirmation.

"Chris, come on, start shooting or get a move on, you know the rules when you're on the court with Travis. Not much has changed in the years you guys have known each other. As for Terra and Grandma, they caused a bit of a scene that day. We were there almost half a day, but it was a lesson that woke us up to how bad Grandma was really getting, and a story we'll have forever. Travis, we really should be getting back inside. The service starts in ninety minutes, and you should get ready and relax." In her soft motherly tone, she also gave me that stare.

We made our way back into the church, where I realized I had worked up a bit of a sweat and needed to freshen up before my wedding. The guys were giving me a bit of a hard time for taking time to shoot hoops on my wedding day. If you know anything about me, though, that shouldn't surprise you. Shooting on my driveway or in a gym has had me late to a numerous number of things in my life. It almost led to my wife and me breaking up. She got tired of feeling second to what she called my first girlfriend, Ms. Wilson.

One Golden Day

One Golden Day

5

*It's All about How You Follow Through in Life and in Hoops—
Well, Any Sport*

Come to think of it, almost any sport is about how you follow through. If you're a golfer, your shot will slice or hook if you don't have a proper follow-through. When it comes to baseball, you're not going to get a hit more than likely if you don't follow through. You're definitely not going to throw a strike or get the ball from the outfield to home plate without proper footwork, and here too you also definitely need follow through. When it comes to basketball—my first passion in sports and life for most of my young adulthood—it's about the follow-through. I have learned this is true in many aspects of life. We must follow through in our commitments, our responsibilities, and the things we have chosen to do. For example, when you're in high school, it's one thing to show up like a batter walking to the batter's box. How you perform is based on the work you put in, how you follow through on that work, and how you commit to that performance and that

One Golden Day

swing.

I learned quickly, especially from Terra, that it's important to push myself and follow through. If I want to be the best basketball player I can, I have to put in the work, not just by practicing in the gym, but keeping up with my health: what I put in my body and how I take care of my mind and stay on top of my studies. Terra really started pushing me hard around seventh grade. That's when our relationship went from brother-sister to best friend, and it's when we started coaching each other to be great. It's not a coincidence that it was around the same time that she and my grandma stepped up at that basketball tournament, showing me how much they cared and how much they were invested in my development and my success on the court.

But enough reminiscing about past days, success, and how I got here. I'm about to get married to the woman of my dreams, a woman that threw up all over me the first time we met.
Little did I know the path my life would take. With basketball especially, and with my wife, it's been a crazy ride from playing basketball in high school at Amarillo High for the Sandies, to W.T. for the Buffs, only to walk on and make the team with Texas Tech and the Red Raiders in the Big 12. I always

outworked, out-hustled, and luckily outshot everyone I came in contact with. People always questioned me about my height. Although I am six feet four inches tall, in today's game unless you're insanely athletic and quick that's almost considered too short. It also took me a while to find my confidence in college. I had some rides to go to bigger programs away from home but wanted to stay close to Terra and my family. In retrospect perhaps it wasn't the best career move. I never thought of myself as an NBA guy, so I was just making the best life decision for me to enjoy playing the game I also loved and enjoy what little time I would get away from it.

"Hey Travis, Travis, snap out of it, Bro. You awake over there?" Chris snaps me with a towel and as I come to I notice my Mom smiling at me.

"Chris, what gives? I was just thinking back, enjoying the moment for a second."

"I know Bro, but we are about to do a toast. I know we aren't about to get drunk in the church, but a small toast to our man getting married. To Travis." Chris pulls out six glasses—for me, my four groomsmen, and one for my mother.

"Chris, I'm counting one extra glass in there. You don't think my mother is about to join in, do you?" I said as I glance at her.

"Travis, my only son, is getting married today. You bet your ass I'm going to take a shot and have a toast on his wedding day."

I know what you're asking yourself, Where the hell is your dad in all of this? Did your parents get divorced, is he dead, is he gone? You've barely mentioned him. What gives Travis? You're being kind of weird about your dad, and we're already pretty far into this story with you.

I know, but my dad lives a complicated life, and we've just learned to live with it. Remember that story I told you about how he had to leave us for work when we were in D.C., but I didn't mention what for? It's because oftentimes we didn't know what for. All I know is that my dad has worked for multiple branches of the government, even DARPA. He started out as one might expect, in the military, with the Army, but didn't take the usual route. He went to college first, graduating top of his class in psychology and criminology. He wanted to specialize in Psy-Ops for the military after school. He ended up getting into counterintelligence and international diplomacy, whatever all of that mouthful entails.

From what I understand, he has been very integral over the

years, working with different heads of state, embassies, and other international agencies in solving various problems and crises. That is why my dad isn't around a lot. It's something we deal with and accept. It's hard not to be proud of a dad like mine, who's making such an impact in the world. It can be hard, don't get me wrong, but he is inspiring in his own right. Now I know I told you my parents are somewhat hippyish in their parenting style, but that's from the viewpoint of a child, not a young adult. They just really wanted us to grow up well-rounded, with a good view of the world. They
didn't want us to be narrow-minded or stuck within the school/work system that is structured to feed school kids into the workforce as good worker bees.

It's not a crazy viewpoint but an observation on the structure we currently have in our society that has progressed over time. As a society in general, we've accepted this, and the few who work outside those confines often push the envelope of success. But I'm done digressing. My parents have always taught us to think outside the box, push the envelope, and see as many viewpoints as we can. I can only assume part of that stems from my father's work all over the globe interacting with different cultures and different people.

One Golden Day

"Mom, I still can't believe you just took a shot with us," I say with a big grin on my face. She's used to having to carry more than one role in our house.

"You know your dad wishes he could be with us. He's stuck on a flight right now trying to get here, as we speak. It's a long flight across the Atlantic. He got stuck doing what he does best: fixing problems we don't want to know about." She said that right. I can only imagine the world he operates in.

"I know. We've dealt with it for so long, but he was so close this time I thought he'd be able to pull it off. Usually he's either here or there's no chance in hell. I think that's what has me on edge." My mom leans in, and gives me a big hug.

She always has that way of just making me feel safe. Terra used to say the same thing, but that's what mommas do best. They show up, they make you feel better, and the world just seems to slip away. Our mom has had no shortage of moments like that. I remember when Terra hurt her leg playing softball. It was a freak accident. The problem wasn't just the accident itself, but when and how it occurred.

See, that year Terra had grown six inches quick. It was one heck of a growth spurt that, mixed with this broken ankle and leg, put her in a bad spot because she would have to spend a lot of time in rehab. I remember being in the hospital, after surgery, seeing her all drugged up, with a cast from her foot to above her knee. Just seeing her with that helpless look, even though she was sleeping, I just felt for her. I could overhear the doctors talking to my mother because my father was gone on another work trip somewhere overseas. They were telling her that Terra should make a full recovery, but a lot of it would have to do with her and how she attacked her physical therapy.

"Mrs. Golden, there is going to be a lot of muscle atrophy when she gets out of the cast, and
damage from the injury. It's going to take time and work for her to get back to full function and agility. She does have age and size on her side. Being petite, light, and young means she should
heal quick and fully, but it will still be a long road ahead." The doctor was trying his hardest to speak calmly to not startle an already fragile mother.

"Thank you, doctor. How long do you think she'll be out from the anesthesia? My son and I could use a bite, at least from downstairs, but I want to be here when she wakes up."

"I'd say you have a few hours. To be safe if you keep it under an hour, you'd have more than enough time either way to ensure you'll be here when she wakes up. It's not a promise, but it's a pretty good medical guess."

"Come on, Travis, let's go get some food. We can talk and walk, stretch our legs, and then come back up and wait for Terra to wake up." My mom grabbed my hand and pulled me out the door.

We made our way down the hospital corridor through the busy hospital bazaar of nurses, orderlies, and doctors moving around in an organized chaos that looked almost like a beautifully orchestrated ballet. The nurses' station was checking charts, pulling vitals, calling out information to doctors and other nurses who were walking the halls, making their way to rooms. Orderlies were moving in and out of the rooms, getting them ready, cleaning them for the next patient to be in or out of. It was a nonstop machine that kept moving. I can only imagine what it was like working in this environment, being around so much energy and liveliness mixed with such a range of emotions. It's so hard to take in at such a young age. There were people filled with hope, joyfully getting great news about cures, while others were getting news causing them despair, dread, and anticipated timelines of planning that they needed to prepare for.

One Golden Day

"Mom, this has been a long day. We've been here since almost eleven this morning and it's almost nine. I know the doctor said Terra will be okay, but I'm tired and just want to get some sleep, but I also don't want to leave Terra's side. Is there any chance Grandma is going to come and pick me up?"

"Travis, Grandma has been here for a while in the waiting room. They just haven't allowed everyone back yet. Once Terra gets up and we visit with her Grandma will stay the night with her so that you and I can get some rest, and I can get you off to school tomorrow. Then I'll be back tomorrow to check on Terra. If anything changes, I'll let you know at school."

"Okay with it being so late, and it being hospital food? Let's keep it simple. I'm just going to grab a turkey sandwich and something to drink. How about you, Mom?"

She did the same. We both ended up eating sad turkey sandwiches in the hospital cafeteria, talking about how long the day was. We also discussed what it was going to be like for the next couple of months with Terra and her recovery and how she was going to react when she got up.

She was pretty hysterical, as expected, for when the accident had happened she was looking at her leg with the bone sticking through it and her ankle a mess. She passed out quickly before the EMTs even made it out to her on the field. Luckily it was a tournament, so there were already ambulance and EMTs at the park. This meant that they got to her quickly, which minimized issues and complications, according to the doctors.

The injury was gruesome, and Terra took it pretty hard when she first laid eyes on it. I could only imagine how she was going to take it when she woke up from surgery and saw the cast. She's a smart kid. She had to know she was going to be in for a long recovery. Even though we're young, we're smart, and she was years ahead of me in that department.

Mom and I made our way back up to Terra's room. By that time Grandma had made her way up there too. It took a good hour or so before Terra woke up, but she finally did.

"Mom, are you there?" Terra said ever so softly.

"Yes, Terra, I'm here, honey. How do you feel?" Mom leaned in and gave her a soft kiss on her forehead.

"My head is killing me, and it feels numb, which I can only assume is a good thing. I don't want to feel it when it's not numb." Terra tried laughing, but it hurt too much to move in any way.

"Hey, Sis, you gave us a good scare. We've been here with you all day. And I'll be there with you side by side until you get

One Golden Day

stronger and back out there." I didn't know what to say; I was just trying to be positive.

"Hey, Travis, I love ya, Bro. I'm just worried about the next couple of days and weeks, then we'll go from there. I have a feeling it's going to be weeks, probably months in a cast before I'm up and about doing too much," she said, faking a smile.

Grandma piped up next. "Alright everyone, that's enough visiting. Terra is going to need to sleep a lot and let this leg and those wounds get some rest. You two get out of here. Let Grandma take care of her. She'll be in good care with the staff here and with me." Grandma was right, it was time for me and Mom to get some rest.

After long goodbyes, hugs, and kisses, we finally got to the car and made our way home. It was one of the longest days for us, but that's the day that changed everything for Terra. After that, her athletic career stopped and her academic life went to a whole new level. Eventually, a few years later, she would push me to new heights in basketball, when Grandma was at that infamous basketball tournament during the summer after seventh grade.

Terra's summer that year after the injury, when she was ten, was rough. It really pushed her. It actually pushed all of us because she got really down on herself, which I can only imagine that for Mom and Dad was even harder. To watch your child, only ten years old, go through such a hard thing was hard. You know, well, you hope they will come out the other end of it fine, but that's what life is: having the faith that you will overcome and survive.

On the ride home, Mom spent a good amount of time talking to Dad, informing him about the day. With the time delay and work he was doing abroad, it was hard to keep him fully updated on what was going on. I could tell Mom was doing her best, but it was getting difficult. She looked to me to keep the conversation going because she wasn't going to be able to handle the silence.

"Travis, honey, how are you doing after this long day? I know it's a lot to watch your sister go through such a rough ordeal." I was also fighting my eyelids right now; they felt like they were trying to close for the night.

"Mom, it was hard at first, especially watching her get hurt, not knowing how bad it was, then hearing that scream and her tears and the other kid screaming for help. That really stuck with me, but once I saw her get help and she stabilized...now that she's in a cast it's about her recovery. It's going to take time, and it's not going to be easy, but one thing you and Dad always taught us is that hard things in life are normal, and not to shy away from them," I said with a smile, trying to reassure my mom.

"That we have, Travis. We've always wanted you to know that life is what you get out of it, but there are going to be rough days, tough weeks, and sometimes really hard years, but that's just the way it is. Thank you for hanging in there all day; I really appreciate it. Your mom really needed your strength today, buddy." She looked exhausted. I could see how drained she was, but she was trying to take care of everything.

"Mom, I know I'm not a fan of it, but why don't I take the bus to school tomorrow morning? It'll give you a little bit more time in the morning, and I can just walk to the stop." I'd like to take credit for this idea, but Grandma had taken me aside and whispered it in my ear.

"Travis, are you sure? I can take you still. I'll probably run to the hospital early anyway." "Yeah, Mom, you're fine. I'll get myself to the bus stop so you can take care of anything you need tomorrow. I'll just be at school and practice most of the day until five. Plus, I can get the coach to bring me home or to the hospital, whichever is easiest. I'll call your cell before practice and figure it out."

I could tell my Mom needed some help, but she, like anyone in her situation raising two kids—twins who were already a handful—needed help. Her husband, our dad, was away from the country close to three hundred days a year, but that's the life they'd chosen. It wasn't perfect, but it was ours, and it was how we functioned. My grandma did an amazing job of stepping up, helping us out, but even she wasn't around full-time because she traveled, had a job, and enjoyed her free time. When she was free, she was all about it, but it was not the same as a full-time support system. This has taught Terra and me how to be self-sufficient over the years. This year was going to be crazy tough on all of us, but we almost always figure it out.

Finally we got home and both of us stumbled inside, went through the motions, and went to bed—at least I know I did. I can only hope mom finally got some rest. I set my alarm to get up early so that I could beat Mom in getting up and try to head her off, keep her in bed, let her get some much-needed rest. That way I could also take care of everything I needed to. At a quarter to six, I heard the alarm on my phone go off, waking me up. I went downstairs to make sure I could turn off Mom's alarm, (again Grandma's idea). I went back upstairs to get dressed, take a shower, and get packed for the day.

I grabbed a quick breakfast, just threw some yogurt into a bowl with some fruit, scarfed it down, then grabbed a bagel and a bottle of water. As I made my way out the front door, I left a note for my mom. I let her know what was going on and headed out. I really hoped she'd have a better day and I really hoped Terra would have as good a day as she could. I was going to do my best to focus on school, basketball, and my tasks because I wouldn't have much help. I knew that that day, as was true for the next couple of days, were going to be a challenge for all of us involved to figure out how, and what, the new routine was going to be. I'd get together with Terra's teachers to see if I could get her schoolwork organized so she didn't fall behind.

About a week went by. Terra was finally home and functioning enough to go from the couch to her bedroom a few times a day. I was bringing her work home and to school, each day keeping her on point. Her teachers said she could make up all tests the following week when she got back to school. For the time being, I was getting her to talk about it, about anything that was hard for her. She was still in a bit of a daze.

"Terra, how was your day? Nine was the usual: class and

practice. You get to do anything new today?"

"You know it, Travis. I tried to use every bathroom in the house, making sure to take my time with my crutches and tour the whole house, not simply moving from the couch to my room." Sarcasm noted.

"Fair enough, that was a dumb question. I'm just trying to keep you dialed in, sorry. Did they give you any follow-up dates at your appointment today?"

"Actually, they said the swelling is going down nicely, which is good. If this keeps up, they might reset part of the cast more quickly than they'd expected. They said because the cast is so big, they might have to re-access it over time. I'm going to be stuck in it for a while, it could be four to six months, depending on how well it heals."

"How are you doing, dealing with what happened? Do you think you'll ever get back out there? Do you even want to?" I keep pushing her on this. I don't know why, I just did.

"Travis, I don't know. I've never been so scared in my life. I never thought I'd walk again, and even though they keep telling me I'll heal, and I'll be okay until I get there, I have that fear every day. Playing sports is so far away from my mind right now."

"Terra, I'm going to keep pushing because I know that's what you would do with me. But if you ever need me to stop, just tell me. Don't yell, don't scream, tell me quietly. If I know you're calm when you tell me, then I'll know it's time, but otherwise I'll assume you just need me on your ass like a good Bro."

"Thanks, Travis. Love you, Bro."

We spent that whole year pushing the shit out of each other, and it was brutal for her. I also had to help her with her studies a lot in the beginning. Many times it was because she'd missed her classes or her physical therapy and other appointments. I learned new study habits that stuck with me forever. I wouldn't be the man I am today without all the experiences I had growing up. I know Terra had a rough time getting over that injury.

It took her nearly a year just to get back to a brisk walk and another year before she could run at a good pace. Still, she kept on a diligent routine and diet to stay healthy. She wanted to keep her mind and body right because she knew her life was changing. Still, she wasn't giving up, and that inspired the shit out of my mom and me for sure.

One Golden Day

It was always hard to gauge Dad, especially when I was a kid because we didn't get to talk to him except in small chats here and there. It wasn't until I was in college that I built a strong relationship with him. He then had a job that had him in the states more, so I was able to communicate with him on a normal schedule. I know it seems weird to say that about a father, but that's how we grew up and the life we lived. My mom played both roles. That's why she took that shot with me, why we were waiting for my dad, and why I was on edge.

You might be asking yourself, Where is your sister in all of this, on your wedding day? That's a different story altogether. But right now, I need to get back to trying to get my mother drunk.

"Alright, Mom, let's not stop at one round. Chris, let's make one more toast just to be safe." My mom gives me a look of death.

"My man Travis, that's what I'm talking about. Line them up. What are we toasting to?" Chris looked at me.
"Let's toast to love—of friends, of spouses, and family. Without it, where would we be?" "Travis, my boy, I couldn't have said it better myself. Come here and give your momma a hug."

One Golden Day

And like that, my mom and I hug for what feels like forever, but I know it's only a few moments. Yet it got me to slow down and realize it was time to get ready and get my mind right for this wedding. I was about to get married to the woman of my dreams; she had chased me all over the globe.

Hey, did I ever tell you how I went from playing basketball in high school, then W.T. at a small college, only to walk on at Texas Tech, and even make a run at the pros. But not before I almost lost the love of my life, Leighton.

6

My First Love, My First Girlfriend: That Relationship with Mrs. Wilson

Ever since I can remember the simple sensation when I'm in an empty gym and...

Breathe

Spin the ball in my hand

Breathe Dribble twice *Breathe*

Then I take a shot and hear the snap of the basketball net from a perfect shot, no matter where I am on the court. That feeling always gets me to a point where I can just forget about all that ails me; where I can just let the world slip away. As long as I can remember, when I had a basketball in my hand, the rest just took care of itself. Some of the best memories I have of my father is him teaching me the proper technique of how to shoot a jump shot. He even sent me videos as I got to high school on what items to work on after watching a game film that Mom had sent him.

One Golden Day

Like most kids, when I started out in my youth, I wasn't always great but I was willing to outwork the other kids. One thing I did have was an athletic ability and aggressive nature. When you're five or six, that's all any youth coach is really looking for because those are the things you can't teach a child. In the summers, because my father would work away from home so much, he would usually get a few different two-week vacations or at least work-from-home stints. The summer between my fifth and sixth grade, he really worked with me on my jump shot, going to my left and really getting aggressive about basketball.

I had already had a passion for the sport and I had been practicing on my own, but it's not the same as having coaching. A coach is someone who works with you on the finer details, giving you drills and pushing you beyond your limits. Without that pushing, it's hard for anyone to go beyond what they feel is possible with *anything* they do. In any job or any skill, we are usually our own biggest obstacle because we lack true self-confidence in our abilities. That's what makes some of the greats so amazing. People like Kobe Bryant who, at such a young age, knew they were great. I also knew they were going to outwork anyone and everyone they would ever come into contact with until the end of their career, simply to be great.

I remember reading a story that talked about him in high school in Philadelphia. He was sixteen, practicing at the 76ers facility with an assistant coach back then. I think his name was Tom Thibodeau, and at the time the coach was working with a young star on a bad team; the young star was named Dana Barros. They were splitting double teams with footwork, dribbling, and pass outs. Kobe watched intently, then after practice asked the assistant coach if he would help him work on the same drills. The coach telling the story raved that rarely do NBA players want to work on those drills, let alone high school players already known to be phenoms. It's that level of dedication I strove for. I pushed myself, for as I grew up as I gained the independence to stay late at school, work in the gym, and work with extra coaches.

Enough daydreaming about what was, what could be, and what could have been. My wedding day is here, I'm about to get married, and I still can't get basketball off my mind. Then again, this is almost what cost me my soon to be wife in the first place. As I said earlier, she used to call it my first true love. My first girlfriend was Wilson, my basketball. I remember the big fight, the one that led to us breaking up in college when I was at Texas Tech. I had been on the team for a year and in the previous year I had been a walk-on with limited playing time. When I was at West Texas A&M I had led the team in most states, but then again, the competition was much easier and lazier. Going up against tier-one talent pushed me and made me feel alive, even if it was a struggle.

"Leighton, I don't obsess about basketball as much as you say, and even if I did, having a passion in life isn't a bad thing. Are you saying it's only a problem because I'm not a starter?"

"Travis, those are your words, not mine. I'm just tired of you moping around when you find out you're not playing in the game again, especially when you know you can outshoot, outplay, and out-hustle half your team. Then I have to deal with your ass and I have too much going on to put up with that crap. I don't know if I can keep carrying your baggage along with mine." She had a good point.

"I came here because I was tired of wasting my talents at W.T. I wanted to push myself and if I failed at least I knew I'd done it by taking a shot and not wasting it somewhere. I'm sorry that it hasn't been easier for either of us, but I was upfront after a few dates that basketball was in my life and has been since day one. If it's too much for you, I'll understand if you want to walk away."

"Are you really breaking up with me, when I'm the one who's opening up to you?"

"You just told me you said you can't keep doing this. What the hell am I supposed to think?" "Don't give up so easy on us. I know you wouldn't give up on old Wilson over there."

"Ha, very cute. You've been sitting on that one, talking shit with your girls? If it's too much to deal with, then walk away and stop with this back-and-forth shit. I treat you right, I love you to the moon and back, and I have a dream. If you can't support me, I'm not going to force it."

"There you go again, Travis, giving up on me. Shit, I feel like, well I don't know, but it doesn't feel great I can tell you that. I need to think. I really didn't expect you to cave so quickly and give up."

She had a good point; I was giving up on us way quicker than I would basketball or anything else, like my family or school. But that's just how I was raised. I mean, watching my mother run solo for so long taught me to be strong and have confidence that you can be okay by yourself. Don't get me wrong, I love her to death, she's my world. I'm also not going to sacrifice or give up on who I am to be with someone, not yet.

One Golden Day

I'm not even sure who I am yet. I'm only twenty years old. Let me first get a legal drink before I start killing off dreams to be with someone I love.

The fight went on for almost two hours and we would make up for a few minutes only to find something new to fight about. Eventually, we both decided to let me finish the season single. I wouldn't expect her to "wait" for me, but I wasn't going to be actively looking either. We took a break from each other, a breather if you may for the next couple months so I could bury myself in my practice, my team, and the gym. That's where I usually felt the most sublime, the most at ease, and it had been missing in me lately. I had been feeling rushed at the gym and clouded at practice. And although I was heartbroken, I had a clear mind and a clear schedule, which allowed me to get back to playing my kind of ruthless basketball. The crazy part is it worked. I played myself into the starting lineup, and as the sixth man, the team depended on me. Still, I was able to finish the season averaging twenty minutes a game.

I lucked out because my first year at Texas Tech was also Tubby Smith's first year as coach for Texas Tech at the beginning of a rebuilding year before they got good. That meant he was looking for guys to work and rebuild with,

One Golden Day

character guys, and I was one of them. It took me half the season, but luckily the team struggled back, barely finishing 14-18 for the season. I was given plenty of minutes to grow. By the time the first season finished, I had averaged 11 points, 4 AST and 4 REB. For me, coming from West Texas A&M, where I was average and in the starting lineup and going up against many different opponents, I was happy with it. But I'll never forget that exit interview at the end of the season with the coach before the off-season.

"Hey, Travis, thanks for coming in, and one hell of a season. I know it wasn't what we had hoped for, but we have a lot to build on next year."

"Thanks, coach, I'm just happy to be here and a part of such a big program. Anything I can do to keep improving and growing with the team, I'm on it. Just tell me what you need and I'll hit the gym off-season."

"I know, Golden, I know. You're one of the hardest-working players I've seen in a long time; you're a gym rat for sure with one pure shot. I know you only have one more year of eligibility left next year, and I wanted to tell you we'd love to have you back. I know you walked on this year."

"Thank coach, that means a lot."

"I'm not finished. We would also like to offer you a scholarship for the remainder of this season, and all of next season, as a thank-you for all the hard work you put in this year. You definitely earned it, son."

"Shit coach…sorry. Thank you so much; what can I do to show you my appreciation?"

"Just keep up all the hard work. Keep it up in school and be a great leader for the youngsters; they need a leader like you. Have you thought about life in basketball after college? Coaching, international, developmental?"

"International? Developmental? I honestly thought of coaching, but with my size, figured no one would give me a shot past this."

"You have a great shot and play some killer defense, Travis. All it takes is one coach to believe in you at the next level. Whether it's the NBA, the NBADL, or overseas, you just need to keep an open mind and keep hustling." Coach put his arm around me, giving me that look of encouragement.

"Thanks, coach, I won't let you down next season and I'll look out for the next guys. You can count on that."

"I know you will, Travis, keep it up. I'll see you in a few weeks."

One Golden Day

Like that, I went from being a star player on a small school to a potential starter with a scholarship in the Big 12. I know I only had one year left to prove myself but to me it was a shot worth taking. The next three months were filled with training the underclassmen, focusing on schoolwork, and getting my left hand stronger. I spent a lot of time working on deep threes, strength training, and endurance to ensure I could push myself to the limit on the defensive end and still hit long threes on the offensive side. But the one thing that kept lingering was my relationship with Leighton. We were still friendly and she would check up on me every few days. We'd even go on casual dates, grabbing a bite to eat or a drink every week or so, but that was it.

I know she still cared about me, and I still cared about her, but I just had to focus on my dreams. If our lives weren't in the right spots, it would be okay; it was just part of life. Not everything that we want to happen will happen. I remember going out to dinner with her about a week before training camp of my senior season. We had been dating on and off all summer but decided to go back on in friend mode for the season.

"Travis, I'm so proud of you and what you've pulled off. What you have accomplished is nothing short of amazing," she said with a soft smile.

"Thanks, Leighton, that means a lot coming from you. I know you haven't always seen my basketball dream the same way as me. Coach keeps pushing me to try continuing in basketball after college, in some fashion."

"You would be amazing as a coach, but I really do think, especially now watching you up close, outworking and outperforming so many of these guys, if you have a great season, I think you've got a shot. I know we talked about taking a break again, but if you're open to keeping it going, I think I'm finally ready to be on board one hundred percent.

"Really? after all the on-again, off-again stuff, you're finally in it no matter what? What changed?"
"Honestly, I think I just grew up a bit and realized you're either with someone or you're not.
 And if you are, you support them with all your might, all the time, especially their dreams."

"Well, I don't know, I had such a good finish to the season last year. Can we ease into this, and just keep things how we are and then go from there as the season starts?"

I know what you're thinking. What are you waiting for? At this point you either love the girl or you don't. This is my dream, my one and final shot to do this right. I want to make sure my mind is right going into this. It's not saying I don't want to be with her, it's just a risk I'm willing to take. I want to put my dream first.

"Yes, Travis, I will support you any way I can, whatever you need. I'm here for you now. I'm sorry that I didn't see this before and we had to spend the last year going through all this..."

I cut her off.

"Let me stop you there. Neither of us was in a good spot, and I needed to get my mind right with my goals in life. I love you to death, and I really do want to spend the rest of my life with you. I'm just scared moving forward that's all."

"I know. And I'm here, either way. Let's just get back into it slow, don't worry about it, okay?"

"Thanks, Leighton. I really appreciate it."

Going into the season we were in a great spot, essentially dating without a title, light stress, limited BS and just supporting each other. It's what a healthy relationship is supposed to be like, I assume. I was still scared shitless about the upcoming season. We had started training camp and the youngsters were stepping up. The coach was happy, saying I'd done a great job

One Golden Day

pushing them, getting them ready, but now I felt bad. I was concerned I'd done too good of a job and put my starting position at jeopardy. Then again, that's always my fear and anxiety just getting in the way.

At practice the coach pulled me aside after I pulled up from a few feet inside half court and shot a few different times, hitting three of five during a scrimmage. I know they were thirty-five feet plus, but I also know it's in my range and it can spread the court out drastically, so it's a great shot for us. Right as he called practice and had everyone leave the court, he called me over.

"Great practice guys. Head into the locker room and get cleaned up. Travis, you stay here, we're going to shoot some free throws and chat." Coach looked at me with a sly smile.

"Oh, coach, what did I do?"

"Travis, when did you decide to start pulling up from damn near half court like that?"

"Well coach, if I'm feeling it, it makes sense, cause it'll open up the defense, spread the floor, and give us an advantage. It's just how I feel. I've put in the work, for the range."

"Clearly you have. Your form is still smooth out there, also great job with the young guys. You did a great job getting them ready, as well as yourself. I could see you have been pressing for a few days but you're finally starting to settle in. I wanted to talk to you about a few things."

"What's up, coach? You know I'm always about the team first."

"I know, Travis. I think it would be a perfect fit to make you team captain. The other coaches are talking to the guys right now in the locker room. I can assume it's going to be an easy sell. Those guys all look up to you."

"You serious coach? I don't know what to say. I won't let you down."

"Travis, I know you won't, but I need you to remember one thing. Winning and losing are different than letting the team and me down. Just stay within yourself, be the leader you are, and the rest will come. Don't do too much, okay?"

"Thanks, coach, I appreciate the trust and the support. I'll take this like everything else and do it with care." And a shit ton of fear. I was shaking inside.

It was right then that the team came running out of the locker room, screaming "Golden." That shit gave me goose bumps. I chose not to play at other big schools, to stay home. I really don't know why, but I did, and thought I'd lost my chance at a big team, a big school or a next step. Now thanks to my hard work and thanks to coach, I'm going to get recognition. More important, I'm going to get an opportunity to prove myself to the basketball world that I belong here.

Even if it is out here in West Texas. The thing is, we will play teams like Kansas and Texas that will have NBA scouts watching their talent. I need to perform all nights, but know which nights to bring it.

After everything died down and the high fives dissipated in the locker room, I went and tracked down the coach one more time to talk to him about something pressing on me. I needed some advice. I know what you're thinking. Why not call your mom; why not ask your sister? But this affected the team and at that moment, that was front of mind to me.

"Hey, coach, can I talk to you for a minute? I just need some advice on a few things."

"Trevor, as captain, you and I need to have open communication. Pull your phone out before I forget, so I can give you my cell. Text/call anytime you need to talk, especially about team stuff. You're the voice for the guys and we need to be on the same page."

One Golden Day

"Thanks, coach, but believe it or not, this is more of a personal nature. But I think it's going to affect the team, so I was looking for some advice."

"What's the girl's name?"

"It's that obvious?"

"Trevor, I've been doing this a long time so what can I say? Let me ask you two very important questions. Do you love her? And does she support you and the dedication it takes to do this?"

"Yes, most definitely, I love her. The second one is T.B.D. We separated and were on and off all last year/season. I played my best ball when we were separated but still close friends. But she has since apologized for making me choose and told me she's now behind me one hundred percent.

"I think that's your answer. The hard part of dating when you're younger is that you're growing up, both of you, so it's not going to be easy. Do you plan on being single forever with basketball? I would assume not, so you might as well learn how to balance the two if you love her, and she's willing to support you. There's nothing stronger than someone with an even stronger partner behind them."

"I guess I never thought of it that way, coach. Thanks, I

really need that. If it's okay, I think I'm going to shoot until my arms go numb in the gym."

"I wouldn't expect anything less of you Golden, that's why we made you captain. You've got that drive so many people lack."

"Thanks again, coach."

Just like that, I walked out of his office, went to the locker room, threw my gym clothes back on, put on my Bluetooth headphones, and started shooting like crazy. I had to work through all of this, and I made a mental decision that I had to decide that night. I was going to either commit to basketball and Leighton or just basketball. I wasn't going to drag it out any longer; that wouldn't be fair to either one of us, especially her.

With each breath, I could feel the sweat running down my brow like a thought working its way through my mind, making its way like the ball does from the boards to my hand, then through my shooting motion. I thought through each fear, of what could be, what would be best for us, and best for her — or was it best for me?

In thinking this through, I'd line up my hips and my elbow and let it rip, then watch the ball fly through the air. As I did I felt the stress leave me, watching those thoughts disappearing into the net.

After two hours of shooting, running, fighting back tears, and screaming at the rafters, I decided it was time to call Leighton. But I still didn't have it in me, so I just texted her.

Hey, can you come up to the gym? I let the staff know you're coming.

Yes, I'll be there in fifteen, is everything okay?

Yes, I just need to talk.

While Leighton was on her way, I stopped shooting and started running stairs for a while, trying to get myself winded, working though as much tension as I could. I knew where I was going with my decision but I wanted to be certain, and I felt that when I was exhausted and pushed to extremes I often did my best work. That's where I find my true self. I have found that's where my character, my fears, and all that bullshit that gets in the way just floats away like sweat
running off my brow, and I'm left stripped to my core—vulnerable and pure.

I was pretty high up, and had a feeling someone was shouting at me. With my headphones on it was hard to hear, so I pulled them off but couldn't hear anything. I started running again, making my way around the concourse, doing wind

One Golden Day

sprints from section to section, then down an aisle, then up another. There it was again. I took my headphones off. *Was Leighton here already?* I know she said fifteen minutes, but I figured it would take closer to an hour.

"Hey, Travis, where are you at?" "Leighton? Is that you?"

"Ya? I'm downstairs in the hallway by the locker room. I tried calling you a few times, but you didn't answer?"

"Sorry, I accidentally put my phone on silent. I'll be down in a minute."

Shit, now I felt a little bit like an idiot, but that wasn't a first for me with Leighton. I always end up acting like a kid around her, putting my foot in my mouth and acting a fool. But my mother always tells me that her favorite part of Leighton is the way she brings out pure joy in me. After talking to the coach and thinking through this, I've decided I need to jump all-in with basketball and with Leighton and see where it goes.

"Leighton, I'm sorry for making you wait, I thought it would take you longer. Were you close to the stadium? I was actually walking by when you reached out; that's why I was so quick. Is everything okay? It's not like you to ask me to come to the gym. I don't think you've ever asked me to come to the gym, especially so close to the season. Are you sure everything is okay?"

I leaned in and gave her the most passionate kiss I could muster.

"I love you, Leighton. I just wanted to tell you that after we spoke the other night, and you told me you were behind me one hundred percent. I didn't know how to take it. I've been so focused on basketball, and what could be, I didn't know how to take it." She was still recovering from my sweaty kiss.

"I love you, Travis. What are you trying to say? You're talking a mile a minute and kind of all over the place."

"I'm all-in if you're all-in, no more of this half in half out. I'm going to commit to you and basketball and learn to balance. If you're behind me, then I'm going to learn how to dedicate and support you just like you are supporting me."

"Travis, are you saying no more games, you're all-in, and you're willing to hear me out when you're being a little crazy? I understand in season, during games, and pregame, you need to do you but you also have to communicate what you are doing and why."

"That's exactly what I'm saying to you, Leighton. Even if I'm swamped with work, I'm going to learn how to communicate better. Just know that when the season is over, it'll be my turn to dedicate time to you, as you have to me."

She leaned in and returned that same kiss back to me.

We spent the rest of the hour just sitting in that corridor, cuddled up and talking. It felt for the first time in a long time that we were both in the right place, coming together. It was one of the best feelings I could remember. I felt solid for the first time. When you keep making big life decisions, changing your path and hoping for the best, there is this constant cloud of uncertainty that lies over you. For the first time in years, I felt like it was coming together. All the big risks were paying off. All the sacrifices and tough decisions I'd made had gotten me to this point with this woman and this opportunity.

One Golden Day

7

Wedding Time and Game Time—Always Nervous

It's almost time for the wedding. I've been nervous before big games, but this is something different. This is more than a game; this is a celebration of something that is bringing the two of us together forever. Now, I'm bursting at the seams. I just want to run out there, grab her, and scream to the crowd she's mine, she's mine forever, and I can't wait to make it official. There have been lots of stressors in our relationship—from my basketball career, family losses, and Leighton pushing to complete her degree. All the time she was trying to support me in my dreams, which actually had been trying for both of us.

At this point Mom weighs in. "Alright, honey, are you ready for this? I know you wish you could have all of your family here, but I'm here, and we have plenty of friends and family out there. And the most important person is your beautiful bride, and she's here grinning from ear to ear."

She has a point.

"Thanks, Mom, and you're right. Instead of thinking about what is and what isn't I'm just going to enjoy the moment and be happy with those who love me and who are here to celebrate this amazing moment with Leighton. And I know Dad should be here tonight, hopefully for the reception." According to our last update that was the deal.

"Yes, last time I got an e-mail from him he was on the plane and about forty-five minutes out, which means he will make it here in time for pictures and in plenty of time for the reception. It is not perfect, but for Dad and his schedule it's almost a miracle."

"Yeah, it is and I'll take it. I'll be so focused on Leighton and Father Dan anyway that I won't even notice anything else. Which reminds me I need to talk to him. Is he still waiting for me over by the door?"

"Yes. I love you, son, I'll see you inside." She gave me a huge hug and a soft kiss on the head.

I still can't believe how lucky I am to have found someone like Leighton, a woman so strong
and amazing, but also whose faults fit in with my strengths and

mine with hers. That's the strength of our relationship now and has been for many years. It's not that we have a false sense of "perfection," but instead we have found a way to work with each other's weaknesses and support each other. For example, Leighton isn't the most organized person around the house, while I have a spot for everything. It's something I picked up from my sister, Terra. Instead of getting upset about it, Leighton does her best to keep it close enough, and I follow through with it.

When it comes to the cleaning though, I'm organized, I don't always clean to completion, probably because I'm always on the run. In any event, that's not the point. I struggle with it, so she keeps it up, keeps it rocking, and I do my best to keep it up too. We work as a team. Instead of getting mad at each other for our shortcomings, we communicate, work together, and try to solve them together. I know it sounds like psychotherapy, but we are in a great place either way.

"Hey, Father Dan, are you ready for this? I know you haven't done a wedding in a while, especially as a Franciscan."

"You know that I am. It'll be fun for both of us, just like our first times. It's been almost twenty years since my last wedding and a few things have changed, so I figure it'll be a blast either way. But let's be honest. Most people out there won't know if I make a mistake," he said, smiling, with a chuckle.

Father Dan is a member of the Franciscan order of the Catholic Church, which takes a vow of poverty and focuses on community involvement, as opposed to the traditional Catholic Church parish builders we are used to seeing or meeting. Father Dan is an old family friend who went to high school with my father and has been a part of our lives for a long time. He stands about six feet tall, and has dark black hair dusted with gray—as if an artist painted it just so. He's naturally thin and carries himself very confidently, which oftentimes grabs the eye of an attractive woman or two, and he has a chuckle about that.

"This should be a blast then. I'll do my best to distract you up there. Did you feel how hot the church is? It feels almost a hundred in there. Then again, it's one hundred and three outside. Whose idea was it again to get married in August? Oh yeah, it was mine."

Hey, it's my grandmother's birthday, it has great significance to me, especially since she's passed on and can't be heard. I miss her a ton and wish she could be here. That seems to be an

One Golden Day

ongoing trend with my family, but I can't really talk. I've spent the better part of my adult life since college running toward basketball and away from my family in so many ways. I made
sacrifices to stay close to home for the sake of the family for the greater good, which is how I almost lost out on so many things. Through sheer will and hard work, I found a way to pull off the impossible.

I would have never thought when I made the decision to play at West Texas A&M for the Buffaloes and stay close to home, and pass out full rides to PAC-12 schools like Colorado, Utah, and a few other schools, that I would have ended up in the NBA. But just like coach had told me when I was at Texas Tech, all it takes is one coach to believe in you—one coach to see something in you and give you a shot. Then you can pull to the next level, especially if you have the talent as well as the work ethic.

Father Dan's voice interrupted my thoughts. "Well, it's extremely hot in here. I'm a visiting priest and I have to use their robes, and all they have are these heavy-ass poly blends. I'm going to pass out," he said with a chuckle, though he *was* sweating.

One Golden Day

"You do look like you're going to pass out from water loss. I'll have one of the guys grab a water for you. Hey, Chris, toss me some fresh water from the cooler over there." Chris chucked it clear across the back of the church, and I handed it off—gracefully I might add.

"Thanks, Travis, that hit the spot. Now I just need to make it through the service without passing out. I think I can manage; you said the reception is open bar, correct?" he asked with his million-dollar smile.

"I forgot that Dad said you guys were old drinking buddies back in the day. Yes, it is. The food is what's going to get you through, though. We're having it at this amazing Italian restaurant called the Pescaraz Italian Restaurant."

We went back and forth for a while. Father Dan did a great job distracting me, even though we were running late. After about twenty minutes, I started asking questions, trying to figure out why we were running late. They told me that she was having some issues with her dress, which I later found out to be false, especially when my dad walked in. Apparently, everyone knew that my dad was trying to make it, even Leighton, and she was okay with waiting until he was able to arrive. It was one last gift of her unyielding generosity to me.

One Golden Day

Even on our wedding day, the day she was the queen, the centerpiece on every table. But she was putting me first for this moment.

"Hey son, sorry I was running late. These international flights over big bodies of water can take a while, did you know that?"

"Dad? What the...?"

"Hey bud, I missed you, and you should thank your lovely bride and mother for stalling for me. We'll apologize to your guests at the reception." He gave me a huge hug as we both fought some hard Bro tears.

"Thanks, Dad, I love you so much. I don't know what I would have done without you here today. It means the world that you're here." I'm blown away by all the love from my family and friends.

"We can make up some time during pictures. We'll just have to get on everyone, push them through, and get to the reception in a timely manner. On my way over here I called a buddy who owns a car service. He's going to limo the wedding party over, taking pictures. He'll bring everyone back as needed to the church, which I figured would be a cool surprise."

One Golden Day

"Thanks, Dad. You know we weren't going for anything fancy, but who's going to turn down a limo ride? Ummm, no one, that's who," we said in unison.

As we walked out together, my father and mother in hand, I watched them walk to the back to begin their procession. I waited on my groomsmen and most of all, my bride. I've only cried at a wedding once. I was at my cousin Geoff's wedding. He had dealt with some rough shit in his life, lots of stress, and some poor relationships when it came to women. He had finally found the most amazing woman; that was his perfection. As she walked down that aisle, he just lost it. His face filled with tears of joy. It was the release of all that suffering, and I couldn't hold it back either. I was so moved by watching the openness, his vulnerability, his expression of pure joy. I just sobbed with him. I remember Terra giving me shit for a good month on it, but I didn't care.

The music started and the procession started and Father Dan and I shared a couple of looks back and forth that could have filled a library of books' worth of knowledge. We were talking back and forth without saying a word as each groomsman and bridesmaid made their way down the aisle. Then there was that pause, that amazing pause in every wedding when the bride gets ready to enter the church.

Father Dan looked at me and said, "Are you ready, young buck?"

"Born ready, Father."

And just like that, the music picked up. Vivaldi started jamming, and I stared down the aisle
looking into my future, past, and present simultaneously.

As I watched her cross the threshold into my view, my breath was stolen from me. I can honestly say that walking onto an NBA court for the first time was no comparison to watching the woman of your dreams float to you down an aisle where you know you will be joined. I've always been spiritual, not necessarily religious. Still, I have faith the two of us will be there until the end because we have realistic expectations for the hard work it will take to make our marriage a success. We just know we want to do it together. We know life will throw us some shit. We've just agreed to share it, that's all.

As she made her way to me, we locked eyes for what felt like an eternity, though I know it was a mere moment. I was lost. I damn near fell over. Chris had to catch me, no joke. There's video evidence of it, so I can't deny it.

"You look amazing, Leighton. I love you so much." As I

took her hand, tears were running down my face.

"You look so handsome, Travis. I love you too. I'm so glad your dad made it," she whispered as she wiped the tear from my eye.

"That was amazing what you did for me, stalling so he could get here, I love you so much."

We went back and forth the whole service. Hey, we hadn't talked or seen each other since the
night before, and Father Dan had to keep interjecting and telling us to quiet down. At one point, he asked the church if we were this annoying in public most days, which made everyone laugh, cause it's true, we are. We are each other's best friend; we cherish the time we have together because we know with my career and her profession it can get trying. But we communicate really well and trust each other. I've met plenty of strong women in my life. Heck, most are in my family, but Leighton has a softness about her.

The service was a mix of Father Dan doing what he's supposed to do, with us acting childish and flirtatious but doing our part. As we finally made it to the end, we got to the candle lighting ceremony. We got teary-eyed, and Father Dan noticed that we needed a minute and took time to do a small prayer so we could compose ourselves. It was a sweet moment for him to share. After the service when he announced us, my heart jumped into my throat, almost causing me to choke. Leighton noticed and squeezed my hand, bringing me back to reality. She always knows where my head is at. Even if I'm playing a game in another city, as long as I know she's watching, I can be certain she's yelling at me with love through the TV and it keeps me going.

"It is my pleasure to be the first to introduce to you, Mr. and Mrs. Golden. We also have a few announcements we must get out of the way. The bride and groom will be doing pictures with the wedding party, then a few with family, and then it's off to the reception. They will keep it quick to keep it on time. They said they will see you over there, for the reception."

Just like that, we were Mr. and Mrs. Golden, forever bound to each other, sync'd legally and spiritually, which I think we already felt. But going through this whole ceremony puts a big bow on it. It brings everyone together, allowing us to scream it from the mountaintop: we have found our partner. I know it's crazy, and I can understand the other side that might be a little jaded, especially with the way my parents operated with the distance between them and all the time that would pass. My parents almost operated like loving, divorced parents.

As I got older, I would talk to my grandmother about how my parents, mainly my mother, made it work. And I remember she would tell me, if you're not knowingly hurting someone, there is no right or wrong way to do life. Just do you, act kindly to those around you, treat others with respect, and the world will survive one way or another. She also used to point out the world had a way of promoting huge assholes to prominence, so being kind didn't always equate to success.

But I knew what she was trying to get at. She was trying to impress upon me that life is what you make of it. We leave a lasting impression on those around us, and it's up to us on how we handle it.

"So, Mrs. Golden, how would you like to come over here and give your husband a kiss for the camera one last time before we head out of here?"

"I think I can muster that. After all, I just married the man of my dreams. Have you seen him anywhere around here?" she said with a laughing smile.

One Golden Day

"Hey guys, everyone, I have a quick announcement. My father made a call and got everyone a ride over to the reception. That means we are heading over there we will be riding in style. That also means no one should be drinking and driving tonight. Let's be safe out there. If anyone needs a ride back to their cars from their house in the morning, just call. Just call us our parents, and we'll help you."

We weren't going anywhere for a honeymoon, at least not quite yet. We had a trip planned but it was just not going to be until later in the year because of Leighton's intern schedule. Oh yeah, I might have failed to mention I'm marrying a future surgeon. She's something, I know. She is working all summer to get her hours in, get her clinical done, and finish up in December. Then come July we are heading out to Hawaii for a honeymoon, just a little delayed—a year. But with my schedule and hers, we have to make it work. We'll be heading out to Santa Fe, New Mexico, for a long weekend, but our real honeymoon vacation won't be for a year. But that's how Leighton and I have always been: we do things our way.

As the wedding party piled into the last limo, Chris got everyone to quiet down for a moment. He then gave a speech that almost brought me to tears.

One Golden Day

"Hey everyone, I need to say something about the best damn friend, bartender, and basketball player from the 806 I could ever call friend and brother. To think that summer you were bartending, thinking about giving up all hope on basketball, life, and everything around you. It took a cute blonde girl throwing up all over you to change your life forever. Not only have you found love, but you also found a wife. I'm so proud to see you play basketball in the pros every night. I'm tracking your career, but also seeing what you two are building with your foundation. I know your sister is so proud. Thank you for allowing me and us into your lives." Chris was fighting back the tears, as was the whole limo.

"Chris, you're too much, Bro. I love you, man. I know, I can't believe it, but that was such a low point in my life, and to have thought that getting thrown-up on was the best thing in my life. If it weren't for that event, my life might have never changed. I probably wouldn't be in the NBA, serious. I love you guys, all of you, thank you for being the best group of friends two crazies like us could ask for." I could barely keep it together, then Leighton started speaking up.

"Chris, Travis, you guys are going to make the bride cry at her wedding, and this isn't good. Come on, you two. I know

One Golden Day

we all have people we miss who couldn't be here, but this is a day of joy, we need to focus on celebrating who was able to make it. Mr. Golden made it all the way from Kashmir. That's insane. We are blessed in so many ways. The tough days mean nothing

because the sunny days block them out."

That's a Leighton phrase. She has a few, but that's one of my favorites. It's true when we have rough weeks, days, or months. We always look at it like laying the groundwork for better days. She has a way of keeping things positive. She keeps it light, even when it's chaotic. She used to stress out, fold under pressure, but ever since that day she called me and told me she was ready, she was in it, no matter what, she's been different. She was ready to commit to me, to us, and everything that that meant. We both decided to put the work in, to support each other, and always be the reason the other one survived their weakest moments. The one thing we do try to work on is the saying that Will Smith and his wife have championed, which is, It's not each other's responsibility to make the other person happy. They bring their own happiness into the relationship, share it, and make each other happy that way. Otherwise, it is selfish to expect someone else to make you happy.

One Golden Day

8

An Injury in Her Youth Foreshadowed Her Adulthood

Terra never was the same after that accident as a kid and not because it took so long for her to rebound. That accident was brutal for her to witness, for her to overcome, and for her to have to deal with. As I got older, I learned about the way she hurt it and understood the injury more. I never could understand how she broke her leg, let alone so badly. It didn't make sense; how did a healthy kid break her leg in so many places while running in the outfield during a softball game? Well, that all changed a few years back when Terra went in for her physical in college. She ran for the cross-country team and the trainer noticed something didn't seem right. Given that she was complaining about leg pain after long runs, they ordered some blood work to be done through her doctor, which ended up bringing back some results that made them run even more tests.

That was a scary day. I remember it like it was yesterday. She walked through the door with Mom, and she sat at the table with her head in her hands. She just sat there and you could tell she had been crying for some time. I could only imagine what about.

"Terra, what's going on? I've never seen you like this. Are you going to be okay?" I sat down next to her and just put my arms around her.

"Travis, I don't know what, I don't know, I can't..." She was just fighting back the tears and couldn't talk.

Mom spoke up. "Travis, why don't you and I talk for a bit? I'll have Dad come in here and sit with Terra." My mom didn't give me much choice.

"Okay, Mom. I love you, Terra. I'll be in the other room with Mom if you need me."

My mom took me into the other room and sat me down. I had never seen my mother like this before; watching her so measured, seeing the way she was breathing shallowly and trying to
compose herself as she was talking to me. It's not like I was a kid anymore, but she almost looked like she had seen a ghost.

One Golden Day

It was just about that moment I lost it and grabbed her by the hand.

"Mom, what is it? What's going on with Terra? I'd say she is pregnant, but you two would be reacting way differently than this, so what's really going on?"

"Your mother would be so happy to find out your sister would be pregnant without a boyfriend at college, instead of the news we just got. Travis, your sister, has been diagnosed with bone cancer. It's a little too early to tell which one specifically. It's slowly been spreading. They think it's been there since her youth and no one caught it. She's always been so healthy that her body just did a good job of fighting it off. But…"

"Wait, what did you just say? Bone cancer? What does this mean for her health long-term? I know she's a fighter, hell she's pre-med, she's going to take this thing head-on." At this point, we were both fighting back the tears.

"We don't know how severe it is, or what the next steps will be. We have an appointment with another specialist tomorrow. Right now, it's just a waiting game. Terra doesn't want to talk too much about it. She just wants to focus on getting through today and tomorrow until her appointment and learning about

One Golden Day

cancer and the treatments so she can attack it."

As I was about to get up and head into the kitchen and go grab my sister, Mom had to stop me and pull me back. She knew Terra and my dad were having some time together and that Terra and I would have *our* time. At that moment, it was about letting Terra come to us individually as she needed us. It wasn't about what we needed, which is always the hardest part when someone you love is going through a hard time.

"Mom, I just don't get it. She was at school running and everything seemed fine. I mean, she got the flu like the rest of us, but nothing major."

"I guess that's what led to it. She was running, got the flu, and the symptoms in her legs kept getting worse. So her trainer suggested a wider blood panel from one of the doctors out there. Then they suggested she come home to her doctor here. That's when they told us it looked like bone cancer; we won't know exact specifics until after she sees the oncologist tomorrow. So today is just a waiting game, hoping tomorrow to get information from the oncologist. I'll tell you more in a few days after some more tests."

Terra isn't the most patient person in the world Mom; she's got to be going nuts. Can she run to clear her head?"

One Golden Day

"That's also part of the problem. Her legs are hurting too badly. That's where this started; where they found the problem. She can't even do some of the things that would keep her calm and focused."

Terra took the injury hard. She had to sit still, stuck in a cast, have minimal movement; well, it was pretty rough all over. But who can blame her—a kid having to go through all that? She was just a kid in her twenties. But from what my parents were saying, they'd caught it early, which was huge. Still, with cancer you never know, not to mention they weren't going to send her home with a death sentence, they knew people were already going to contemplate that. They were going to keep it as positive as possible until they could confirm the worst.

The next three months were a blur, well, at least for me. I can only imagine that for Terra, especially with all of our conversations, it felt like years. That's because she was dealing with it all and trying to wrap her head around all the diagnoses from the doctors. The problem was that her test results were troubling the oncologist and they couldn't tell how severe the issue was. They wanted to keep retesting and sending her back in for more. Eventually, they just decided to do exploratory surgery to see how bad it was. To get a closer look since the tests kept coming back inconclusive.

I remember one instance when she came back after the oncologist had indicated that the tests were inconclusive, which drove my sister nuts. She came home, crying her eyes out. My mom didn't know what to do and she began yelling at me.

"Travis, gets in here; I need your help with Terra! Can you just try and get her calm, she's going to need more tests. They don't know what's going on. They still aren't certain how bad her cancer is and your sister is beside herself."

"I'm on it, Mom. I think I know exactly what to do."

"Oh you do, do you?" my sister said with a shitty look as she wiped her tears away.

"Yup, the same way you stepped up with me in middle school with Grandma at that basketball tournament. I got your back. We're going to figure this shit out, and if we have to find you a new doctor in Dallas, I'll drive you myself." She's always been my biggest supporter so I figured the least I could do, especially in the off-season, was support her.

"Okay, you have my attention. What do you have in mind?" I got Terra to calm down and sparked her interest, which was a start.

One Golden Day

"Let's grab the big dry-erase board we used to use and start researching. From there, we'll see where we end up."

From there we went upstairs and grabbed the big dry-erase board and easel. Yes, we have an easel around my house. We used to use it for family game night but mainly for big school projects. Let's be honest here. Mainly it was Terra who used it for projects. Still, there was one
time she convinced us to play a family game with it, I think, just to show she wasn't the only one using it.

In any event, we spent most of that night using the Internet to find as many different solutions to her issue as we could. Many of them pointed back to her diet, which didn't surprise us because she had an odd diet, but also pushed herself to the limit, which can cause a lot of issues on these tests.

More than anything, I was just trying to keep her mind moving and give her options, places for her mind to run other than the worst place possible. I thought if I could give her a plausible explanation of why all these issues were happening and find a ton of reasons why, even if they were long shots, it would help to ease her mind. It worked, for it did allow her to calm down, and after a couple hours working on it, she finally crashed a little after midnight. I remember heading downstairs and catching Mom, who was still up waiting to talk to me, mainly to check on how Terra was doing,

"Hey, sweetie, how's Terra doing? Is she finally asleep?"

"Yeah, Mom, she finally passed out. She was calm the last hour or so though, which was good. I think all the things we looked up put her mind at ease until the next test and meeting with the specialist."

"Thanks, Travis. You know you're a great big brother. How's the off-season training coming along? Are you excited about your third season in the league? Your father and I have always been proud of you, but what you have been able to accomplish is nothing short of amazing."

My mother was talking about how I had earned a spot on an NBA summer league team with the Dallas Mavericks after I graduated, then was signed by the New Orleans Pelicans and given an opportunity to play in the NBA D-League. Due to some injuries and some great play on my part, I was promoted to play and haven't looked back since. Playing in a blue-collar city has been great because as the coach puts it, I'm gritty and I play crazy defense. I also have a bit of flair for the dramatic when I start pulling up for threes from forty feet. But I've learned where my sweet spot is, where I can operate in the league, and what my skill set is. I've put in countless hours in the gym focusing on my lateral movement, watching film of the opposing teams to learn defensive schemes, and shooting the ball until my arms fell off. I know I have to put in more work than others to stay in the league, and I'm okay with that. The world isn't created equal. I can either figure it out or sit home and wish for it.

I remember reading an article about the former NBA player turned coach and now commentator Mark Jackson. When he was with the Indiana Pacers, he would finish games and get on a treadmill and run for miles until he was exhausted, pushing himself. He knew he was never going to be the fastest guy or most athletic one out there. He did know if he was one of the most conditioned guys, he would have moments where his conditioning would allow him to outperform other players. The league has a way of giving opportunities to people who can find their edge and use it. It also has a way of washing you out fast if you don't find it, so you better not waste your time while you have it.

"I know, Mom. It's been a lot of work, but that's one thing you have taught me, never to shy away from the hard work and to always make sure I'm working harder than everyone else. Otherwise, what's the point?" I said with a smirk.

"You know it, son. If you're going to do it, you've got to put in the work. Otherwise, you might as well stay home. Don't give yourself the excuse. You are talented enough and have the tools to play in that league for years to come. It's up to you to give yourself the edge to outperform."

"Mom, I don't need to be pushed, any more than I already have been but I do appreciate you pushing me. I know you're afraid that I'm going to give up this opportunity again like I did before."

"Travis, last time you had to deal with issues and this family you decided not to go away to school, and almost lost all chance at a career in the sport you were born to play. You have sacrificed so much, and I know you would like to be here while Terra fights this. Eventually, you will need to get back to your team and focus on the upcoming season. You know that don't you?"

She had a good point. "Yes, Mom, I get it. I'm not that young kid anymore who's going to make irrational decisions based on emotion. I'll do everything I can to be here for Terra and you guys, but I know I have responsibilities now."

"The important part is that even Terra knows this, and she

more than anyone is your biggest fan. How is Leighton doing with all this? I'm assuming by now you've reached out to her and told her what's going on?"

Mom knows me too well. "She's worried, same as you, and doesn't want me overthinking it."

"She knows that you're going to be torn between being there for Terra, putting in the work you need to, and being there for her. But she is one of the most selfless people I have ever met. She'll be in your corner no matter what, and that makes your mother very happy."

"Thanks, Mom. Having Leighton in my corner has really helped me continue my run at this basketball career. There's only a few hundred spots and I'm not about to let mine go. I've worked too hard to let it slip now."

The next hour or so, my mother and I spoke of what life had been like since moving to New Orleans. Leighton and I were doing great. She found a great job working at a clinic on the west bank in New Orleans. We live closer to downtown and her commute is kind of a pain in the ass, as she likes to remind me, across the bridge. She loves the difference she gets to make in the community out there. Most people, when they come to New Orleans, think of the French Quarter as the only part of

One Golden Day

New Orleans. **[AU: I took out two sentences of confusing text]**

We have a great place in a neighborhood right off of Frenchman Street, which is just outside of the French Quarter proper. It's where the best music is played in the city, at least that's what I'll tell you. I've been lucky enough to see people like Harry Connick, Jr. and Kermit Ruffins, and even my favorite, Trombone, who plays there. They'll just pop into one of the local joints and start playing. One of the other great things about where we live is how close we are to the stadium; I can ride my bike to it, which is awesome.

Leighton loves the city for all that it offers—from the food to the people to the art scene. Most importantly, she has a huge heart and donates her time all over the place. Leighton studied medicine at Texas Tech when we were in school and has used her degree and license to the benefit of the city of New Orleans. She started by donating time at one of the clinics in town just one day a week and now is working full-time to support and manage a series of clinics. With the two of us being in New Orleans, we are really trying to embrace the city and all it has to offer. Most importantly, we want to make sure we are leaving a mark on the city for the gifts it has given us with the team and this opportunity.

One Golden Day

"Mom, tomorrow is going to be a long day, especially for Terra. Why don't we get some sleep?"

"As long as you're going to, then I'll go. Tomorrow is going to be a long day."

The next day was filled with more questions than answers; tests to better understand Terra's prognosis and long conversations with the doctor that didn't really lead to anything other than more questions. It took almost two weeks until we were given a solid prognosis from the doctor as to what was going on with her and how they were going to attack it. But that was just the start of it all. It wasn't about to change. Just like any disease or cancer, there is no simple solution. Each person is different, and their bodies react to treatment differently. For example, the first couple of treatments that they tried with Terra had adverse effects on her. She was reacting negatively to the medications. Some gave her rashes, and one even made her so nauseous she couldn't eat for a week. She ended up losing so much weight they had to take her off of it.

The next year her cancer was rough on everyone. It was trying on the whole family, but

believe it or not, Terra and I excelled at it. She buried herself in

One Golden Day

her studies and went back to school. Work was out of the question so she focused more on academic endeavors and research. In contrast, I buried myself in the season with the Pelicans. Terra and I talked and texted nonstop. She helped me with the breakdown of other players and scouting teams we'd be playing coming up, anything to keep her mind off of what was in front of her, especially on the long nights. I got her the NBA ticket package so she could keep up with my games and she ended up watching half the league games.

Because of all the help she gave me, the distraction from my own insecurities, and the extra time I would put into the clinics and fundraising with Leighton, I had a full schedule. That was one of my best years. It even led to me signing a long-term contract. It was nothing crazy like you read about those big stars, but something that would keep me in New Orleans for five more years. I told my agent I'd rather have stability and longevity over a few extra dollars, and he understood completely and got the deal done for me.

So full circle, that year almost led to Terra losing her leg, but luckily didn't. It was an option that was brought up more than once. Eventually, they found a treatment that worked, but she still had to drop the track team in college. The disease took too much from her, the strength in her leg, and her whole body. The team and university were so supportive and because of her grades and degree they just changed her scholarship to academic.

Now I know what you're wondering. How was she still at Texas Tech while I was in the NBA? Well, she redshirted her freshman year with track and was on the school program that put her a year behind me, which is how I ended up in the NBA before she graduated college. But watching her from afar, also knowing all the stress and pain she was going through, was rough. I was watching my twin go through something as brutal as cancer, at such a young age. As a kid, I
watched her struggle with an injury that took a long time to heal, and it brought up all those feelings of guilt and sadness.

I remember a long talk we had the night before I played a home game in New Orleans against our hometown Dallas Mavericks. She was trying to give me notes on the team I was going to play. Still, I kept trying to get her to talk about her treatment and recovery, and she kept trying to get me back on basketball.

"Travis, it's about time you called me. I've been waiting for your call since four this afternoon. Hasn't practice been over for

One Golden Day

a while?" It had been; she knew my schedule to a T.

"As usual, you're right, Terra, but I had to get some treatment for tightness in my back. All this extra practice and tension has me a little worked up." Stress can really tear a body up and that particular season had been very rough.

"You okay, Bro? You've never really had back tightness before."

"Yeah, I think it's from all the travel, and getting used to this brutal schedule. I'm not getting much sleep lately with everything going on. It'll just take some time for me to settle in. I'll be okay. How are you doing and how's your treatment going?"

"With your game tomorrow did the coach tell you who you're guarding yet? With the way the Mavs have been playing D lately, you should be able to get your shot off easy and find a rhythm early."

"Sis, that was some major league deflection. Come on, I know you don't like talking about it, but I want to know how you're doing from you, not from Mom or Dad."

"I know, but I'd rather talk about your game tomorrow. As for me, I'm doing okay. It's going to be a waiting game with the current meds and process, and we won't know one way or another until it's either great news or too late. I just try to forget about it. I hope you can understand that."

"I guess I can appreciate that approach. I can understand that, but you're not only my sister, but my twin, and I worry about you. There's something different to being a twin. You know that it makes it even harder knowing I'm out here playing ball, living my dream, while you're going through this nightmare." Not to mention, it reminded me of when we were kids all over again.

"Travis, we can't change what's in front of us, we can only do our best to handle it. Mom and Dad always taught us that. If we make excuses or feel sorry for ourselves, we'll never get through it, or we'll miss an opportunity to survive it. I'll be okay. Just like I was as a kid, it sucked, but it gave me a new path and a new personality. We'll figure it out; we always do."

She was right.

"I love you, Sis. I feel helpless sometimes and want to fix everything for you. Speaking of Mom and Dad, how are they doing with everything? I know Dad is working closer to home these days, but Mom's got to be driving you nuts. I mean, as a kid you almost killed her."

My dad hadn't done international travel since Terra got

diagnosed. He had kept everything domestic and tried to keep everything a car ride away. That way, if anything changed or turned into an issue, he could be back the same day. I know to some that might seem obvious, but my father's job has always been an important one. It was a choice my parents made to keep us in West Texas and not move to D.C. or New York, which would have made his travel schedule easier. They figured he'd travel so much that our lives should be thought of first. It's a decision Terra and I are grateful for every day.

I loved growing up in the panhandle of Texas. There's something to those sunrises and sunsets, that wide-open feeling, opportunity, and vast greatness upon you. I didn't truly appreciate it until we moved to New Orleans, where the city is on you. People are everywhere. The culture is amazing down here, with the cuisine and music that makes you feel like you've traveled to a different country. Still, there is something about growing up where we did that gave me the perspective and work ethic I have.

When Terra was injured as a kid the first time, my mother didn't take it well and she got overly protective. She was always running around, trying to cater to Terra, which drove Terra nuts. Terra was like me in that the more she felt helpless,

One Golden Day

the more frustrated she felt. Even if it was going to take an hour to get to the kitchen to get a bowl of cereal, she was going to do it herself; she didn't want someone else to do it for her. Some might call it stubbornness; I call it a strong will to persevere.

Terra really struggled that year, but just as she did when she was a kid, she found a way through it. She ended up beating the cancer. They found it early enough, but said there was a chance it could come back. However, with regular checkups she should be fine. As she used to say, "fine" is a degree of perception. She ended up graduating with a second bachelor's degree and even passed her MCAT first try with flying colors. It was after this issue that she changed her specialty. She'd originally been interested in becoming a registered nurse or general practitioner in medicine. But she decided to study oncology and focus on research. After that day, everything changed—the way I approached basketball, my marriage, and my family—because I realized you never know what tomorrow may bring.

9

5 Minutes an Eternity – Those Two Little Words

We were still in the limo, making our way to the restaurant and my new wife was curled up on me just enjoying the moment while our friends were partying. We'd had a great conversation with Father Dan in the back of the church that put the rest of the night into perspective. This was one of those moments that made his words ring true. I remember he kept saying it, over and over, it was almost like a mantra.

"Terra, Travis, come here, let me talk to you two really quick before you head out of here."

Father Dan had this aura about him when he called you. I know we had just been married and had those goose bumps all over and the day felt like a blur, but he still had that presence about him. When he was in a room or was talking to you, he received your full attention. It was a gift; he probably would have done great with any profession he chose. It's amazing he went down the path he did, or perhaps it was due to the grace of God, as he put it, that he was given a chance to inspire so many.

"Yes, Father Dan? Are you going to reprimand us for playing around too much during the wedding?" Leighton joked with him.

"I'll take accountability. I was already amped up and full of the giggles before the wedding started. And I'm not mad at either of you, I simply wanted to take a moment and talk to you about something very important. Now that the wedding is over, now that you are about to go to your reception, I wanted to give you some advice about the rest of the night."

Where's he going with this? I wondered.

"Father Dan, not sure where you're going with this, but you know we've lived together for a few years now," I said with a smile, then got punched in the ribs by Leighton.
"Shut your mouth, Travis Golden, let the man speak."

"Thank you, Leighton, and that's not where I was going with this, Travis. I wanted to remind you that tonight is going to fly by. It's going to be one of the fastest nights of your life. The wedding ceremony is one of the longest hours of your life. It seems to hang there forever, like the morning dew on a spring

One Golden Day

morning created by artists. But the reception tends to turn tides, go another speed altogether, so make sure and take time to slow down, slow down, and I repeat, slow down. Most importantly, enjoy it and embrace these moments that will be with you forever."

As we sat there in the limo, watching our friends enjoying the night, having drinks in the limo celebrating our wedding with us, Terra and I locked eyes. Both of us realized what Father Dan had just spoken to us about earlier. He was trying to explain to us that this moment would run by fast, so we should take some moments to talk to embrace and hold hands. I know that we've been together for many years, but you only have one wedding night, so make it count. It was some of the best advice I had been given in a long time. And it wasn't just about that night but something that I took with me moving forward in my life for many years to come.

Leighton leaned into me as she had so many times before, curled up into my arms, and snuggled under my shoulder, which took my breath away. As we pulled up to the restaurant, we told the wedding party to give us a few minutes alone in the limo, which went as well as one might expect, when my best man, Chris, chimed in.

One Golden Day

"Alright, everyone, let's give Leighton and Travis some private time. They need some private time, they don't think they can wait until after the reception," he said with a huge grin on his face, aided by a few beers.

"Very funny. We just want a quiet minute alone before the craziness continues. Thanks, guys," Leighton said, blushing a bit.

Just like that, we were alone in the limo. We turned the music down, slowly syncing our breathing and becoming one and the same. It was a moment that you rarely get; it was the calm in the eye of the storm. As we sat there we could see everyone enjoying themselves inside the restaurant, and the wedding party making their way inside with drinks in hand, partying it up, smiles all over. It was everything you would expect, but there was still something missing.

"Travis, what are you thinking about right now? I can always tell when you're pondering something."

"I just miss Terra, I wish she were here. It's hard not having my sister here on such a big day. I know you and I have been together a long time, and our wedding almost seems like a formality at this point. Not to mention I've missed so many big events and tough times in her life over the years, but it's just

One Golden Day

hard. And I'm trying to take it all in like Father Dan said. Enjoy it."

"It's hard to enjoy it when you miss someone so much. It *can* be hard, I know you miss her, and you miss your grandma. That's why we tried so hard to make sure your dad was able to make the ceremony; I know it would be worth it."

"That was special and thoughtful of you as always. I love you so much, Lei."

I only call her that in the small moments that we share, the quiet moments at home, before bed, when we're alone together. No one else really knows it, I don't know why. I don't even know when it started, but I've done it for a while now, and I love the way she looks at me when I do. Until she stops looking at me that way when I say it, I'm going to keep doing it.

"I love you, Travis, I know we never do anything the normal way, but it's what works for us. Hell, you made it to the NBA, I'm helping run clinics in New Orleans, and we're two kids from the West Texas panhandle. I'd say we're doing okay." She's got a point, and she usually does.

"I know, but it doesn't make it any easier for us to go through life knowing we keep putting ourselves in these situations. Away from friends and family, although I know, we've made great friends already in New Orleans."

"I don't know where life will lead us. All I do know is that I'm happy doing it with you, being there with you, and solving the chaos with you. The rest is secondary. You're my partner, my rock, and I can't see myself going through this crazy life without you. I love you forever, Travis. Thank you for making me the luckiest girl alive."

"Right back at you, Lei. I love you."

I couldn't help but notice that she was holding something back, which was odd for her. She's usually open and talks freely. I also noticed that neither one of us had had a drink that night, which wasn't surprising. Since I'd been playing in the NBA I was so picky about everything I put in my body. Leighton is a health nut and she rarely drinks anymore, not even wine. This was going to be a fun night of watching our friends and family get drunk while we probably sat back and relaxed, enjoying maybe one drink or two, if any, and just watching the show.

"Ready to go in Travis? I think we've let them wait long enough. If we keep this up, they might think something was going on in here."

"We should start rocking the limo for a few minutes before we go in. I'm kidding." Right then, she slugged me again in the side, well deserved.

As we walked into the restaurant, I was met with a huge hug by my mom. I was damn near knocked over, and so was Leighton by her parents. I know I haven't talked much about her family, but they are quiet and keep to themselves. They aren't much a part of our lives. They aren't bad people, just hard to get a hold of. Leighton doesn't like to talk about it, so I don't press

it. It's the only thing she hasn't been an open book about our whole relationship. She confided in me her feelings toward them and told me how hard it had been growing up, but wouldn't go

into too many of the experiences. She harbors too many poor feelings and inviting them to the wedding had been a big step for her. She was now trying to mend fences. Since we don't live here anymore, we figured it might be an olive branch to start some form of a relationship with them.

From what little I do know, her parents weren't mean to her. They were merely absent. What I mean is, they did the bare minimum as parents. As soon as she was old enough to fend for herself, they reminded her daily that she could take care of herself, and she should take care of herself. They claim they did

One Golden Day

their best, gave her a home, and that should be enough, but any kid can look at what other kids grow up with and get upset. I know I would have, especially growing up the way I did with the mom and grandmother I had and even with a father who traveled as much as he did. He provided for us, putting us in a situation to rarely if ever be wanting.

I can only imagine growing up in a household where your parents almost look at you as a burden, and then remind you daily of that burden as you get older. Leighton explained to me that growing up that way and living in and out of different apartments—knowing that it was a game to see if they were going to get kicked out—was draining. She never knew if she was going to be at the same school long enough to make friends. This led to a lot of the trust issues in the beginning of our relationship. Once she worked through that, and we had long conversations about where they came from, we were able to come together and really push forward. That night she and I had sat in the gym at Tech after I had shot baskets all day and talked to the coach, she and I had discussed this very thing. That's how she had finally come to that conclusion: she realized the root of it, and where it came from.

My grandmother used to tell me that we can't choose our

parents, and there comes a moment in every kid's life when they realize their parents are no different from those of the kids they went to high school with. Their only difference is that they had a head start in life, and they had you. It's true. Don't get me wrong. Most of us look to our parents with reverence because of what they do for us, but that's not always the case, and that especially rings true in those moments.

"Travis, what took you guys so long out there? You guys enjoying the married life a little too much?"

"No, Mom, we were just taking some great advice from Father Dan and taking a little time for ourselves to enjoy the night for ourselves, that's all."

She looked at me and smiled. "Father Dan is a smart man. Glad you did it, now let's get in here and celebrate. There are a lot of people who've traveled a long way to see you two."

Before we could sit down and try to enjoy even a few moments in the restaurant, my mother started shuttling us around from one family to the next. There was a small announcement of us
entering the restaurant, but it wasn't a big party with a dance floor and DJ, as many might expect. It's not what we wanted. It was more of a large dinner with a crap ton of friends and

One Golden Day

family. The night was a blast, but it was quick. Just as Father Dan had told us. I felt like every time I looked down at my watch because it felt as if thirty minutes past every single time I looked, after a while, I was afraid to look down and check.

We had some great conversations, though, and I got to meet some of Leighton's family I had never met. Especially since she doesn't talk much about them, it was nice getting to know them, but I do understand a little bit more why she is guarded about them. If you compare the way we were brought up with the way she was, I can see why she has craved our family events and steered away from hers. More and more as the night went on I could see that trend growing.

After a solid hour of talking to her family and friends and watching her joke around with her maid of honor, Colleen, her best friend since middle school, I was starting to feel like I was watching a movie of my life. I kept trying to slow down, but the more I was aware of the night, the quicker it went.

There was one point that we got sucked into a conversation with my Uncle Steven, who is a bit off his rocker. We ended up talking politics and walking the line of some racial conversations that kept making Leighton and me a bit on the uncomfortable side. Though we both grew up in West Texas, we never saw the world or people as anything other than that. Especially me being a white basketball player, I realized quickly, especially in college, that I was a minority in my profession. I had to learn to pay attention and learn from others who had grown up differently from me. When we moved to New Orleans, that was one of my and Leighton's favorite parts: the vast difference in cultures and ethnicities all over the city.

Uncle Steven kept bringing up immigration and other crazy shit at our wedding, and eventually, Chris came in to save the day. He got him to take a shot with him. That was essentially three hours, me and Leighton calling in our best man/maid of honor to bail us out of awkward conversations.

That was until we both realized we were starving from not having eaten all day.

"Leighton, I'm starting to get hungry, are you doing okay?"

"I'm okay, but yeah, I could use something to eat. Want to head over to our seats, and grab some food?"

Just like that, I waved Chris over for some help running interference so we could make our way to the table. He was good like that; he had no problem acting a fool if needed or playing the role of bouncer if needed.

"Alright, everyone, we're going to give the bride and groom

some time to sit down and eat.

Let's all take a few moments and sit down as we start our speech. I'll be the first to go, then we'll have Leighton's maid of honor unless she wants to break the ice first." Just like that, Colleen stood up and took the mic from Chris.

"Don't mind if I do, thank you for that great introduction, Chris. Give a round of applause for such a great speech by the best man, short and sweet. I kid."

I'd only met Colleen a handful of times over the years because she went to the University of Texas in Austin and Leighton went to Tech. What I do know is how sarcastic and witty she is. Her speech followed suit and started off just the same. She was driving the room like it was the White House correspondents' dinner. I'm pretty sure she used social media to do some deep dives on people and pull stories. She was telling stories on Leighton and me but was also pulling out stories from my parents, her parents, and even friends of ours who I didn't even know she had met. She crushed it. That's when I remembered what Leighton had told me: Colleen had gone to school at the University of Texas, theater. She wanted to be a comedian, a writer.

"That was amazing; not sure how I'm supposed to follow

One Golden Day

that." Chris stood up as the room was still cheering

"That's right guys and gals, let's give it up for the amazing Colleen. She will be here all night before she has to run back to Austin to finish her studies in psychology and veterinary science.

Also known as the study of men." I did my best impression of a comedian.

"Thanks, Travis, for trying to lighten the mood, but I think I can do my best to follow the greatness that was Colleen's epic speech. Did anyone get that on video so we can post it and try to get that shit viral?" He had a point.

Chris's speech was heartfelt at times, but mainly the usual Bro code best man speech one has come to expect from Chris. He's a linebacker with a heart of gold. You can always count on him to help you when needed. He would help you mend a fence clean out the gutters, and be a shoulder to cry on, he's the best, the best man a friend could ask for. Even though he's still in

Amarillo and I'm in New Orleans living my best life, he's still helping my mom and my sister a ton. He's always there for us. I'm lucky to have such an amazing team in my life.

I know what you keep thinking. Where is Terra, why isn't

she at your wedding? That's a long story, and we'll get to that, but for now let me enjoy my wedding.

"Leighton, are you doing okay? You look a little flush, is it because we didn't eat all night?"

"It's been a long day, we haven't eaten, and it's a lot for one day. I think I just need some food and a little sleep later. I'll be okay." Just like that, she and all of her ladies got up for the bathroom.

"I mean I've seen that in the club, but at a wedding? Every girl goes to support the one girl going to the bathroom? I hope everything's okay, what do you think, Travis?"

"Yeah, she said it's just been a long day for both of us and neither of us ate properly, so we're both running on fumes. Luckily, we don't have a honeymoon coming, just some rest and heading back to New Orleans in a few days." Chris is always looking out for us.

"You know I'm always worried about you two, especially since I don't get to see you anymore unless I'm watching you on TV. Which was weird enough when you were playing for Tech, but now watching you in a Pelicans uniform is just crazy. So proud of you, Bro."

"Thanks, Chris, it's been a heck of a ride, that's for sure. I

One Golden Day

can't imagine it without Leighton or the family and friends I have around me. I just wish things were a bit different, but you know that."

"I know, man, but I did have some role in that, we all did. There's not much we can do about that anymore. We just pray, hope for the best, and see where time gets us. Only time will tell."

"I know, but I still wish she were here. Not sharing this with my sister has been one of the hardest things I've ever done. I can't imagine…"

Right at that moment, I heard a commotion at the front of the restaurant. I hadn't noticed when Leighton and her bridesmaids had gotten up that they had made their way to the front door. But now I was really confused because I heard screaming, crying, and what seemed like something good. Out of nowhere.

I heard my mother say. "Leighton, how did you, what did you do?"

"Mom, I'm sorry if you guys don't want me here, I can leave." Was that Terra? "Travis, Get over here."

"Hey, Bro."

10

I Didn't See That Coming; Why Does That Keep Happening?

How did I explain to my sister what happened and what was about to go down? Well, let's see, there are so many moving parts I don't know where to start. I guess we can do this in a few different parts. I'll start with the wedding planning. When Leighton and I were trying to put our wedding together the topic of my sister came up.

"So where are we with your sister? Is she going to come to the wedding if we invite her?"

"I honestly don't know. The other thing is, I don't even know where to send the invite these days. Last I heard she was somewhere in Europe doing research."

"Really? Wasn't she on the East Coast somewhere last time? When did she end up overseas? I can never keep tabs on Terra these days." No one can, that's kind of the point.

After her run-in with cancer, Terra didn't take it too well.

One Golden Day

She was determined to ensure that she would stay in remission and if for some stroke she didn't, she would have done one of two different things: found a way to kill it the second time around or make a big enough impact in the cancer community and the research that she wouldn't feel her time was wasted. From the time she was diagnosed until the time she finally was in remission, Terra was on a mission. She completed her schooling, MCATs, and her requirements to become a practicing physician. Then she decided to go into research. She made sure to maintain clinical hours to keep on it and worked at an ER a few nights a week, but spent most of her time doing research. She devoted her time to her work.

I feel like she got her sense of service, her sense of being a part of something bigger than herself, from Dad. After watching me leave to go on and chase a dream, she tried hard to fight for hers, even if it changed over time. Eventually, she became a machine, driven and cold, which is what led to a lot of the issues that we have today. She would tell us that we didn't understand what it was like, that what she was doing was more important than anything we could ever imagine. She and my dad still talked a little bit, which I'll get to in a minute.

Her research has taken her all over the United States.

One Golden Day

However, it has pushed her to the outside of the United States because of the limited laws or less restrictive rules they put on research facilities in different countries. One of the leading facilities in Europe and the world is in France. Last I heard that is where she was currently working, but I hadn't heard from her in almost a year. "When's the last time you reached out to her, Travis? I mean, really tried reaching out to her, with a call or text?" Leighton asked me one day. This was assuming her number even worked anymore.

"I'm pretty sure it was our birthday, so almost a year ago. I know it's been a while, but I'm getting tired of no responses." The truth was that I tried almost every month but I got no response, and I'm a bit ashamed my sister wouldn't even respond to me.

"If anyone understands family trouble, you know it's me," Leighton told me. Your dad was always on the go. Now that he's retired and home with your mother, you and Terra are out in the world traveling. Your mother is in good hands, but I know it's hard not talking to your sister for such a long time, especially when you were so close."

Not to mention I had my worst season yet, not poor or bad enough to get me kicked out of the league, however. Still, I have

One Golden Day

progressed every year in the league, gotten better, and this year was the first time I struggled more than I progressed. I had some injury issues, and it would have been nice to have my sister to talk to, share with, and cry with.

"How did you even find out where she was? I swear the last I heard she was still working at John Hopkins doing research. When did she go overseas, and where?"

"According to Chris, she moved to France to work at some research facility for a six-month stint. While some of their research continues on a joint project they are working on it. He said it's not common to get them to work together, but you know Terra, she always finds a way."

"She's still talking to Chris and your dad, at least there's some contact back home. Is that how you get your information, mainly through Chris?"

"Over the past year, since their little fling, yeah, that's about it. I always had a feeling they would end up dating at some point, but I didn't think she'd end up hurting him. She really did a number on him, essentially telling him work was always going to be her priority."

"I mean, my life was rough. Your sister had you and your mom, not to mention your grandma. How did she end up so hard, cut off, and distant? Do you think it's really from the accident as a kid and eventually cancer just pushing her to a dark spot?"

Yup, timing is everything. "I really do, she always struggled when it came to stress, the really hard stuff. She didn't run from it, but she did sometimes cave to it. She was afraid, would shy away from the tough days. I think she has found some strength and control in the work she is doing. I understand it, but it doesn't make it any easier."

I really do understand it. I get it. I can see how she got from that scared girl on the softball field to the cut off distant driven researcher traveling the world trying to push cancer research to its limit.

She has broken down research barriers that existed all over because people were afraid to share data or cross boundaries. Or they were just simply afraid to lose funding for their projects if they worked with competing scientists. Even though so many people wanted to work as a team, it was a race for so many of these companies. These funds are invested in the research. That is why the funds are not tied to profit. When people can share data and work to solve problems and not be afraid of losing out, we can achieve great things.

One Golden Day

As her brother and her friend, I am so proud of her and the work she was doing, I just wished she would let us be a part of it, even just a little bit. If not, her work, her life. Maybe a call on a Sunday for five minutes would go a long way, but again I also get it. I'm sure she felt like the world didn't stop for her as a kid when she broke her leg and again when she was diagnosed with bone cancer. Why should she wait for the world? She was playing catch up.

"I know you love your sister. You should keep trying until you get through. If it was reversed you know she would do the same thing."

Leighton was right. "I know, I promise I'll put more effort into everything with Terra, but for now, let's focus on the rest of this guest list. I noticed you only wrote about ten names under your side and about forty people under mine, what's with that?" If we're going to do some family digging...

"You know how I am with my family; we don't have a big family first of all, and the few friends I have are going to be standing up at the wedding. I really don't even want to invite my parents but figured it's an olive branch, an opportunity to try and show them I'm willing to try."

"I know that's what it looks like, but the question is, are you

One Golden Day

really willing to try? I know there is a lot of resentment there. I'm not sure one day can wash all that away."

That conversation about her parents went on for about two hours, but it wasn't surprising. A few times we went off the beaten path, talking about Terra and her situation. Leighton was brought up by two parents who struggled to survive—and having a child was a struggle. That wasn't the biggest issue. It was more the fact that they liked to remind her as she got older that she was a burden, that she needed to find ways to be self-sufficient. I couldn't even imagine growing up in that kind environment, what it would do to one's psyche and development in character.

My sister always was one wanting to solve the problem, but she's not the person wanting to be in the middle of the problem. That was me. I was the person chasing the storm, getting into the middle of it, and she was researching it, keeping me alive. That's what made us such a great team, and it's why I feel so lonely some days, though I'm happy with my wife, happy with my team. Not having my sister around, my twin, can be so empty. Just having those conversations that only we can have.

I hope I can find a way to get her to our wedding. It's already going to be hard enough not to have my grandmother, who we lost years ago, there. Chances of getting my dad in the country are going to be a pain. However, he's been domestic lately, you never know, he's always one crisis away from getting called into action.

"Do you think it'll help if I try and reach out to her? Not sure it'll make a difference, but I can try."

"Go for it, Lei. I'll try anything at this point to get my Sis back, especially to our wedding."

There you have it, my sister was gone, she was not around anymore, she was constantly on the road. I up and left to join the league. Still, I was home in the off-season and saw the family when we played in Dallas or OKC, and even flew them out to New Orleans a few times a year when we had long home stands. I called or texted daily with my mom and dad. I used to talk to Terra daily, then it became every few days, then once a week; it kept getting less and less before I knew months had gone by.

As for the Chris and Terra relationship, last Christmas when Terra was almost in the clear of all her cancer, Chris was over and they stayed up late talking. They had always been good friends, because we had been good friends and Terra was the female version of his best friend, and an attractive female,

One Golden Day

so I'm told. It's not surprising that they fell for each other. The crazy part was I thought if it was going to happen, he would be the one to take advantage and she would get hurt, not the other way around.

Chris fell hard for her, and got close fast. They'd known each other for years, and he connected quickly. After about three months, Terra got a clean bill of health and was almost done with all of her clinicals and she was about to find out her next step. Without even talking to Chris, she took a job at John Hopkins in Baltimore and acted like they were just a fling, and it was no big thing. Chris tried to play it off, but you could tell it was rough; he took it hard.

From that moment forward, though, Chris and Terra kept in close contact, and he became the Terra spokesman for the family. She wouldn't even talk to Mom, which was nuts. She only talked to Chris and occasionally Dad for travel advice, especially now that she was overseas a lot more. But most of her conversations or relationships seemed to be function driven, meaning what could she get out of them and did they serve a purpose? Don't get me wrong, I don't mean in a selfish, dirty kind of a way, but more along the lines of a pragmatic, scientific way.

One Golden Day

Everything to Terra became a problem to solve, a plus-minus in what she could gain. I get it, especially with the way we were brought up, watching Dad be gone all that time and Mom just finding a way to make it work.

Leighton added her invaluable advice. "Okay, I'll reach out to her a few different ways and try the old, 'I'm the bride it would be a great honor to have you' routine. Let's see what we can pull off. I'd love to have her here; she's your sister, and going to be my sister-in-law."

"Thanks, Lei, I appreciate the way you always try to help keep us together. I know you didn't have quite the same upbringing as we did. Though ours wasn't perfect either, we did find a way to still be supportive. Even now, we love Terra and support her. We just miss her, that's all."

When it comes to family, you just love them, you find a way to make it right, you find a way to make it work, no matter how stressful, no matter how crazy. I remember the day I found out that she and Chris had been sort of "together." You can't even call it dating because they wouldn't go out on dates, they just hung out at the house, did stuff with the family, and I'm pretty sure hooked up like wild animals in heat. Though no one wants to think of their sister like that, I can imagine the stress. The mental drain of being locked up and dealing with all that bullshit that comes with cancer….to find relief? An escape like a fling would be heaven no matter how short.

I could see how Terra was surprised that Chris fell for her. Most of the time, he and I were friends, and he was hanging around us. He never had a long-term girlfriend. He wasn't a one-night stand kind of guy, but I'd say it felt like he had a ninety-day rule, even if it wasn't written down somewhere it just kind of happened naturally. I honestly don't know how to explain it. It's not like Chris was picky or was trying to push people away. We would ask him where his girlfriend was, and he would say, "Oh, we don't see each other anymore," and after a while, we just stopped asking because we'd figured out it had run its course. That's why when Chris and

Terra started hanging out, Mom and I thought it would be perfect for Terra. It would be something fun for her. Chris would go through his usual routine, and we'd figure out the rest on the back end. He never spoke ill of his ex-girlfriends, and we would see them time and again. None of them showed a bad bone toward him; it's like he was just that kind of guy.

When he and Terra stopped seeing each other, we didn't think anything of it, but then one day, my mom saw that Chris

One Golden Day

was kind of moping around the house. She asked him if he was okay and he played it off. She approached him, got him talking, and realized he had fallen hard for Terra. Probably because he knew so much about Terra before they started hooking up, it made that three months seem longer than anything he had ever been in before. Still, he really took it harder than Terra did.

"Speaking of Chris, how's he doing with Terra? I know they are friends and all, but I know he still has feelings for her. It's got to be hard to be in that situation, being someone that she confides in, knowing she isn't going to return the same feelings," Leighton asked me.

"I don't really know anymore what their deal is. I know he took a couple trips out to see her when she was in Baltimore. They say there are just friends that make it work their own way, but who knows? I remember my grandma used to say, "There's no right or wrong way to do life unless you're trying to hurt someone else on purpose." She was a smart lady who kept it short.

It's crazy to think that it took a year to go from here to her walking into the reception a few hours after my wedding. Apparently, Leighton didn't want to say anything because she wasn't sure if Terra was even going to make it. She made it sound so open-ended that Leighton didn't think she was going to come.

One Golden Day

"Hey, Bro."

"Hey, Sis."

"Sorry for not reaching out lately, we've both been kind of busy." "Terra, it's okay, you don't need to explain."

"Actually, there is, there's a lot to explain to you, to Mom, and especially to Chris."

"What are you talking about?"

"I'm pregnant."

11

Two Words Can Carry So Much Weight

"Wait, what did I hear?" In unison, you could hear my mother and Chris; they were in awe.

If the topic wasn't so serious, the event, my wedding, and the woman saying she's pregnant, not my sister, I think I'd be in the corner right now wishing I had some popcorn to enjoy the show. Instead, I got to deal with the chaos. The emotional rollercoaster that was a wedding was about to get hijacked. "Lei, did you have any idea about any of this shit?"

"Um, no. She barely committed to coming. I wasn't even positive she'd gotten the invite or the date of the wedding. Not to mention I would have said something, that's info is too good to keep from you." Leighton sucked at keeping secrets.

"Sis, do you know who the father is? I guess it's not my

One Golden Day

place to ask, I'm just wondering." Chris stared at me like I had just crushed his soul.

"That's an easy one. I've only been with one person in the past six months. Chris, remember when you came to visit me before I left for France?"

"Terra, are you telling me what I think you're telling me? Am I going to be a dad?"

Just like that, the two of them disappeared off to the side and started talking. My mom, Dad, and us (me and Lei) started talking too because you know, we had all just found out that Terra was pregnant with my best friend's baby. We were all clueless to any of this. It was one of those moments in the movie when the actor looks directly into the camera and just gets a glossed over look of confusion.

"Mom, with all the health issues, the meds she was on, and the chemo, I thought they weren't sure she could even have kids, at least not for a while?" I looked at my mom; I was so confused.

"The doctors said that the side effects of all the meds, mixed with the chemo, could lead to her having issues related to her ability to have children, as well as other issues female and otherwise. I'm not sure how detailed you want me to get?"

One Golden Day

"I got the picture, Mom, that's I guess why we're all surprised."

"I'll bet you're not as surprised as she was. I wonder how she even found out, if she wasn't expecting to have a period or anything." Leighton had a good point.

Yeah, I mean, how did she figure that out? Not to mention how far along was she. I didn't even notice or get a good look. She came in quick, had a ton of people around her, and took off to one of the side tables so she and Chris could talk. I mean he's a good dude who has had a spot for her in his heart since she ran off. I could only imagine what must be going through his head right now. I know he just wanted to be a good dad first and foremost. He is a great bartender and can pretty much work anywhere, even overseas. He'd just need to learn a new language. Before I could continue my thought, the two of them came out to join the rest of us.

"Mom, Dad, and everyone, let me first start off by apologizing for everything and how distant I've been," Terra said to the assembled party. "I know I didn't handle the cancer well, or what it did to my psyche, but I really am happy with the work I'm doing and how I'm making a difference. I just need to be better at being a good sister, daughter, and friend."

One Golden Day

"We love you, Sis, so it's okay. That's the best part of being a Golden, we're always here for each other. Good, bad, indifferent, even if you show up after a year, pregnant with my best friend's baby."

"Travis, watch your mouth, come on."

"What Mom, too soon? I'm just trying to lighten the mood a bit, and let Sis know we're good at the same time." Judging by Terra's smile, I knew we were all good.

"We're good, Bro, I love you; wouldn't want you any other way. As for Chris and me, we have some stuff to work through. I think we know what we're going to try and do. Don't worry, Mom and Dad, we're not going to rush in and get married, but Chis is going to move to France to be with me and he'll find a job there while I finish up my work."

"All I know is that I want to be there for both of them, no matter what, I'm not going to label it or expect it to be perfect. I'm just going to be the best I can for these two." Chris was glowing.

Just like that, we all came together and gave Terra and Chris a huge hug. Our wedding just went from being a wedding to a family reunion/baby announcement in one quick moment. The best part was Leighton, and I couldn't have been happier to have the attention off of us. This allowed Leighton and me to just sit back and watch people talking to Terra about her work, the baby, and everything else. I was pretty excited for Terra and Chris, because I knew he'd be a great dad. He's the kind of guy who can adapt anywhere, even if that means bartending in France so that he can help and be there for his family.

Terra mentioned that when Chris visited her before she left for France is when it happened. According to Terra, that would mean that she got pregnant almost five months ago. She was pretty far along. That means this baby is going to be due pretty soon, which means she could already know its gender.

"Hey, Sis, if we're doing the math in our heads correctly—and we're all doing it—that means you're about five months along. Doesn't that mean you can or do know the sex of the baby?"

"Wait, what? You mean you know what we're having already?" Chris was a little shocked.

Terra quickly spoke up. "Slow down, I haven't done any tests yet for that. I have an ultrasound tomorrow at two. I might find out, do you want to go tomorrow, Chris, if you're free?" Leighton was fishing to see how dialed in he was.

"I'm pretty sure I'm scheduled to work, but that's an easy

shift to switch or cover. If I call my boss and tell him why I'm sure I can make it. If not, I'll still be there. I wouldn't miss it for the world." Chris was still beaming. It made me wonder if that's how I'd be when or if I had kids.

I mean, Leighton and I have had the talk about it, but with my schedule and her career in the clinics, we've been a little bit afraid to. I know she's also afraid because of how she was raised. She would be an amazing mother, she has such a kind heart, a loving and giving spirit. I would love to watch her raise a family. My only fear is her putting her career on hold. She does so much I wouldn't want her giving any of that up. Then again, if Terra could pull all this off, it might be the inspiration we needed to go down that same road.

"Leighton, so what do you think about all of this? It's our wedding, and Terra comes in here with this news, almost hijacking our wedding. At least it was at the end of the night, but still."

"Travis, you know I could care less. We had our day at the church, now we celebrate and visit with friends and family, the rest is secondary. I'm just glad she made it and that there's a chance of mending a relationship."

As usual, Leighton does have a point: getting close to my

sister again would be huge. I do find it funny that there is some major symmetry to her ending up in France and me in New Orleans. With New Orleans having such a huge French history and foundation, she *would* one-up me and go where it all started.

"That's true Leighton, I just want to get my sister back. This looks like it might be the beginning of the start of that. How is everything with you though? I feel like there has been something you've been holding back all night. Was this it? Were you wondering, waiting to see if Terra was going to show up?"

"It's a long day, with trying to get your dad here, your sister here, dealing with my family stress, and wanting it to be a perfect day for us, I think it all just got to me a bit. My favorite part of the whole night was when we said our vows, played around up there like kids, then when we took a few minutes to be quiet in the limo, just the two of us. That's what it's about, the two of us being together as one." I couldn't agree more.

"I know, Lei, you really are the best thing in my day, and it takes a ton of support to get me through the day, given all the goals I'm trying to achieve. I know you that understand that, and I'm blessed to call you Mrs. Golden. Thank you for being

One Golden Day

my rock."

I'm reminded about a conversation I had with my grandma shortly after a breakup with a girl in high school. It might have even been my first serious girlfriend — well, the closest thing to serious I ever got in high school. I remember sulking around the house, and I hadn't shot baskets in almost three days. My grandma pulled me aside and gave me one of those talks that sticks with you.

"Hey, Travis, what's going on? Want to go shoot a few, I'll rebound for you. I know your mom and Terra aren't around. I'm tired of seeing you sitting around here, time to get up."

"No Grandma, I'm good, I just want to sit here and watch TV for a while. I'm just not in the mood." I was in a funk, bad.

"Not in the mood, Travis Golden? When have you ever not been in the mood? Once you get a shot up, and hear that net snap, you'll be in the mood. Let's go, I'm not taking no for an answer. No need to change, just go as you are."

I was chilling around the house like your typical teenager, wearing jeans and my favorite beat up NBA T-Shirt. It was an Atlanta Hawks shirt; not sure why I love it so much. It just fit me right, felt right, and had lots of miles on it from me shooting. That, mixed with some slides, I was looking like I was ready

One Golden Day

for a day chilling on the couch, not a session shooting.

"Okay, Grandma, I'll come for a few shots to get you off my back." I knew she wouldn't stop.

For an older lady, she still had the right amount of snap on her passes; they always hit me in rhythm too. Then again, she's been throwing me these passes as long as I can remember. She always knows how to get me out of a funk.

As the first pass hit my hand, my footwork started to fall into place: left foot, right foot, knees bent, explode up into the shot, then release.

"There ya go, that's it Travis, doesn't that feel good?" She knows it does, I'm already smiling. "You know it does Grandma, thanks for getting me out here."

"So, what have you laying around the house like a sloth for three days for? I know you're not sick. Is this about that girl you saw for a little bit?" She knows it is, but she's fishing nicely.

"Yes, I just don't know what to do. I'm used to hanging out with her, calling her and doing those things with her. Now that she's not around, it just feels weird."

"Let me give you some advice. It's going to be hard advice, but you need to hear it. You know

One Golden Day

how hard it is to deal with your dad being gone all the time, but you figured it out, so did your mom. Life is about adapting, whether it's a basketball game for sixty minutes or the rest of your life. You need to make adjustments. If you're getting beat to your left, you can't just give up and let someone drop fifty on you." She had a good point.

"I hear you, Grandma, but it's easier said than done. How do I get to that point? How do I go from here to there?"

"Well, let me ask you a question. How did you get good at shooting from thirty feet away? It took time, right? You took steps, started close, worked on it, then eventually the small shots became easy, and everything was second nature. At that point you didn't even think of the work. Relationships of all kinds, whether it's me when I'm no longer around, or another girlfriend—that hardest part is that initial routine. Still, eventually, you will adapt, you will persevere. You have to believe and trust in yourself."

"I see what you're saying. Each day things get a little easier. There's no magic pill that makes it go away. It doesn't get simple fast, but it gets a little easier each day."

After twenty minutes talking to Grandma, I was shooting, talking, and working through so much shit it wasn't just about

One Golden Day

my ex-girlfriend anymore, but about so much more. The stress of school, fear of basketball season, issues with friends, we covered it all—it was a therapy day that was much needed. We were out there for a good hour and a half. Just shooting and talking. I wasn't doing a ton of running around on account of the sandals and jeans, but that wasn't the point. It was the rhythm of dribbling and shooting, mixed with my grandmother's calming tone, hitting me with a pass and a question, one and the same. Then I would coil up, think through it, release the shot, and let it go. With each passing shot, I was able to release a little bit of tension, until I felt like months of stress had been lifted off my shoulders.

That day I learned how to deal with stress in a healthier fashion, but it's also where the habit of working out stress began, whether it was earlier that day before my wedding or the day we found out that Grandma had passed away. I dealt with my stress on the court. Terra, until her leg issues and bone cancer, would deal with her stress by running or burying herself in her studies/work.

What does this have to do with the day that was my wedding day? On that day I found out my sister was pregnant and my wife was my rock. Well, it's simple. My life is stressful.

One Golden Day

The career I have taken is a ton of work to stay in; even the most gifted have to put in work. There are only a handful of players who get the benefit of the doubt. The rest of us have to work our asses off. Having someone like Leighton in my life is the support system I used to have with my mother and my grandmother. They would work with me, help me deal with the stress, and remind me not to take myself too seriously, focus on the little things, and just enjoy the ride.

Because I had strong women in my life growing up, I have found an amazing strong woman to support and challenge me. Now it's my turn to support and work with her in the next phase of our lives. I can't wait to start a family with her. I'm sure part of these feelings are coming up from seeing Terra pregnant and watching Chris beam with joy. It's infectious to see two people who have been seemingly stressed, apart, and distant come together and try to make it work. Granted, they have a strong relationship, deep friendship, and now they have an even stronger bond that will bring them together: a child. That doesn't always mean that they're going to be happy. Just look at the way Leighton was raised. I know I keep bringing it up. Still, it goes back to the phrase my grandmother would say, As long as you're not doing anyone harm, there is no right or wrong way to do life.

"Terra, do you have a minute to talk? I know you have been talking to Chris and Mom a ton.
But I'd like a few minutes."

It's a pretty normal part of our routine that whenever there is big news, we wouldn't talk about it until the end of the day. It started when we were kids. We would get sent to our rooms for the night, and we would talk about everything. As we grew up, it became part of our routine, our ritual.

"Travis, you know I do. I guess I'm always used to us getting together at the end of the night.
But that won't happen with you and Leighton leaving, for obvious reasons," she said, smiling.

"Terra, I just wanted to say congratulations. Though I know it's not perfect, Chris will be an
amazing dad; you know he will. And I miss you, Sis. I know I could have reached out more, but I still miss you." I leaned in and gave her a huge hug.

"I miss you too, Bro, I know it's not perfect, but I do love Chris, always have. It's actually what he and I talked about when he came to visit me in Baltimore. We're in a pretty good place, this just kind of speeds up that process. He's actually been learning French for me, just in case it was the only way we could be together. He's such a sweetheart."

Chris never told me that. "You serious." I shot Chris a look; he looked confused. "He's learning French, that's awesome, I really am happy for you two. How long are you in town for? Leighton and I have to leave in a few days, get back to New Orleans. I have some work at the facility I have to do with the team; maybe we can grab lunch?"

"I'd love to. How about you and Leighton have a great rest of the night, you and I can catch up tomorrow, either before my appointment or right after? Sound good?"
"Love you, Sis, sounds great."

As we were hugging it out again, Chris walked over, gave Terra a hug and a kiss, and looked at me.
"Hey, what was that look for a minute ago? Did I do something wrong?" "You mean other than knock up my sister outside of marriage?"

"Yeah, other than that. I figured it was something different since you didn't punch me in the
first five minutes of hearing it."

One Golden Day

"You are correct, sir, it's the French thing. Are you learning French? I didn't know that." "Why would you know that? It's not like it would come up in our conversations."

"Still, I love you like a brother. She's my sister, and now you guys are moving to France for who knows how long. It's just a lot to take in."

Before I could get too emotional, Chris started to get everyone riled up.

"Hey, I just realized we haven't made a toast to Terra being home for the first time in a year, the news of a new baby on the way, and the fact that I'm going to be a father. Raise your glasses, guys."

12

Winding Down; Where Has She Been All This Time?

The night was back on track and everyone was having a great time. It was awesome to see Leighton, my mother, and Terra sitting down talking about what I can only imagine were baby things and France. I have heard that France has some of the best public healthcare in the world. At least she's got that going for her. The baby and the mother will get proper care. It's not like she'll be working in some third world country putting herself or the baby at risk. I was just sitting in the corner by myself when I noticed Father Dan and Chris walking over to me with drinks in hand. They know I don't drink much, but when I do, I'm a fan of gin on the rocks with a lime.

"Here you go, Brother, a drink for you to sip on while we sit down and go over the craziness that is your wedding; the day that will go down in infamy."

"Let's get a general recap here. Travis shot some hoops in the parking lot, got married, his dad made it in from overseas, and Leighton surprised him again with Terra coming into town. She surprised all of us by informing Chris she was pregnant with their child, and she's due in like five months. Does that sum it up, boys?"

Father Dan did do a great job summing it up. He also was sipping on a martini, very dry. He jokes that he drinks gin straight with a few olives in a martini glass to feel fancy. He feels the vermouth takes away from the gin. But he had a point on the highlights of the day; it *was* a bit crazy. That's kind of the way we operate as Goldens: nothing is ever quite easy but never that hard either. We just roll with the punches and enjoy the shit show when it arrives.

"The word of the day for me is *success*. I feel the day had a little bit of everything. I can't complain, I got my sister back, married the woman of my dreams (I hope), and my best friend,

One Golden Day

Chris, is going to be a dad. I can't think of a day with more amazing blessings."

"That's a great way to put it, Travis. Your grandmother would be so proud of you. Is that what put you out in the parking lot this morning in a tuxedo, shooting hoops?" Father Dan was still surprised at my weird habits.

"A little bit. I was missing her and I was down a bit. My mom knew I was going to. She already had a backup plan; she knew just what to do."

It was a crazy day, I wish Grandma were here to help us get through the chaos, but I feel she was here a few different times today. Her spirit and spark can be found in Leighton in so many ways. I see it every day, and it brings me peace; I know that I'm in good hands. Just being around her makes me want to be a better man daily. I know at this point I'm talking like a newlywed, but what can I say? I did just get married and find out that my twin sister, who has been estranged for a year, is pregnant with my best friend's baby.

"Hey Chris, I can guess how you're feeling because of what you've been saying. I haven't asked you outright how you're doing with all of this. Where are you two at and how has this past year been? The way Terra made it sound, you two are doing better than any of us realize."

"I'd say that's a fair comment to make Travis, we are in a pretty good place. She may have been distant from you guys, but she always took my calls. The hard part for me was she made me promise to keep our relationship apart from you and your family. She didn't want to keep putting me in the middle of everything. However, there were things that she would let me tell you guys. Now that she's here making amends it's different, but the past year has been rough. I've had to keep secrets from my best friend and his family about their daughter, a woman I love."

If you put it that way, it almost sounds like a Greek tragedy. Falling in love with your best friend's twin sister, only to have to keep secrets from him and his family for over a year to salvage what little relationship you have with them? The more I talked to Chris about this past year, the more respect I had for him and the level of love and commitment he had for Terra. I just hope she saw it too.

"Chris, if you don't mind me asking, what gave you the commitment and level of faith that it will all work out?" Father Dan was doing his fatherly deeds.

"Honestly, faith, plain and simple. I know I love her with

One Golden Day

all I have, and that we will make it work. She is the most amazing woman in the world, and I will chase her halfway around the globe to France to make it work. I think living in France for a period and raising a baby while she tries to cure cancer and improve the world is a pretty kick-ass thing."

"I mean, if you put it that way, it's hard not to pull at my heartstrings, and you got my sister pregnant. I know you would marry her if you could, I'm just giving you a hard time."

"All in due time, at this point. I'll just be happy being a part of her life and that of our child, no matter what it is, as long as I'm there," Chris said with a smile. "What's the plan at this point? If you've been studying French and you're planning on moving to France, even if temporarily, I'm assuming you're going to try and get a job at a hotel or restaurant while you're there. Still, your plan has to have more to it than that, doesn't it?

"I don't think so. I figured as long as Terra's there, I'm working, and I can help raise our child and support her while she does her research. The rest is secondary." I'd never seen him so calm.

Terra and I are planners. We need to put the work in, see the data, and work to improve the results. Chris is just there, willing to flow like a river down a bed, he will adapt to whatever surroundings may come. He looks so calm it's infectious. First, it was his joy that brought me to a new level. Now seeing him calm and collected, simply happy to be in a place where he could make a difference, is good enough. I really think that going into this year, I need to focus on that approach to life—particularly as it relates to basketball and my wife. If I'm going to grow as a man, a husband, and eventually a father, I'm going to have to lean on the things I've put the work into and spend some time on the new ones.

For example, on the court I know where my strengths are. I can keep putting in work, but I'm not a rookie. I'm not trying to get there; climbing the mountain is different than staying on it. I need to focus on maximizing my energy and utilizing it for my family because I want to be there for them. I know it's just Leighton and me right now, but someday there will be more to our family then that, and I don't want to wait until it's too late to be present in my own home.

I know my father sacrificed for the greater good. My mother supported him, and in a way, Leighton and I will go through a similar life. The difference is I won't be overseas, hopefully. We will be together much more, and I need to continue to keep working toward those goals: the ones of a sustained life for our family. Basketball won't be forever, it will only be around so long. Making a positive impact is huge to both Leighton and me but there comes a time when we will need to devote time to children and a greater purpose.

"Chris, for someone going into a situation with so many unknowns, you are handling it with such grace and elegance. May you stay blessed and clear of mind as you work through the coming months."

"Thank you, Father Dan, I appreciate that. I just hope to keep it all together on the rough days. Today is a good one, and I'm going to hang onto it for when those rough ones come along. It's like a night where you shoot 1 for 15. It's rough, you put the energy you have into the defense, get your team involved, and remember the games you put up thirty, knowing you can get it back tomorrow."

"Travis, it always goes back to basketball for you, doesn't it?" At this point, Chris and Father Dan were laughing at me.

"Travis, we've talked plenty about Chris, what about you and Leighton, your beautiful new bride. How are you guys enjoying New Orleans? I heard you recently got a new contract, keeping you there for a while, congratulations."

One Golden Day

"Thanks, Father Dan, it's been very good for us. In NBA money, the contract is what we call a team-friendly deal. However, in Golden family dollars, it's still amazing, so we will be ecstatic to stay in New Orleans for another five years."

If I'm lucky enough to finish this contract out with the New Orleans Pelicans, it will put me with an eight-year career in the NBA, all with one team, which is extremely rare. But when you look at the relationship that my wife and I have made with the team, the city, and the overall impact we've had, it's a win for all of us. That's how both sides looked at it when we negotiated the contract. It was more than just a basketball move. We head up great PR for the team, the NBA, and the community—a great fit all around.

For example, through some of the NBA programs, we crossed paths with Leighton's clinics and some of the kids she works with. When the kids went back to school, we put on a big program to get underprivileged kids ready for school. Her clinics get them the shots they need, we work on getting them clothes, shoes, and school supplies. It's a great program for us and the city. I'm blessed to be in a city with such amazing things to it like the St. Louis Cathedral, the French Quarter, and little holes in the wall like the Kenner Fish Market. The food, people, and culture are one in a million. I can only imagine the life Terra gets to live in France. I hope she's taking it all in when she's there. I highly doubt that she is, but with Chris there I know she'll finally get to see the sights, sounds, and smells of France.

Sitting there with Chris and Father Dan, I was just enjoying myself, enjoying the moment, and letting my imagination run wild, dreaming of a family with Leighton. But all in due time, as Father Dan had said. However, I couldn't help but let my imagination run wild with all of the news that had come that day. Imagining teaching my kids how to play sports, read, learn their colors, and watching their mother inspiring them to be great.

"Hey, honey, come over here really quick." Leighton waved me down. "Go on, your woman is calling." Chris gave me a nudge, the little shit.

"You better get used to it, you'll be getting yelled at in French *and* English soon enough."

As I made my way over to my bride, she had this glow about her. I could put my finger on it. It was the smile she was radiating—her beauty had always taken my breath away. But the day your love chooses to marry you makes it official, it just changes something. It's like someone put on spotlights to your

One Golden Day

love and turned them on full blast for the world to see.

"Lei, you are beaming. What are you ladies talking about over here?"

"Just sit down next to your wife, that's all I want. I would like my husband next to me. Is that okay?"

I can dig it. "Yeah, I think I can swing that." As I sat down next to her, she started to whisper in my ear. Hey sweetie, I'm going to tell you something, but I can't have you say anything, okay? You can't react, you need to just play it calm. I need your game face on."

She rarely did this to me, but when I heard her ask me to put my game face on, I knew it was a big deal. I wondered what she was about to tell me. Knowing her, it was going to be something simple though, like she loves me. That day was the right kind of day for that. Ever so softly, she whispered in my ear. "I wasn't going to tell you anything, but after tonight I really feel I need to, I want to. I took a test this morning, and I'm pregnant. Your mom knows, and that's it, she was there with me. I haven't gone to the doctor, and it could be a false positive, but I think we might be pregnant."

WHAT?!

13

What Is It With Two Words Today?

I'm sure I look like a deer in the headlights, but I was doing my best to work through the Rolodex of excuses if someone called me out for the odd look on my face, from the news Leighton had just whispered into my ear. Mom knows the news, my sister Terra is confused, and Chris and Father Dan are a little drunk and have no idea, especially given the comment Chris just screamed across the room.

"Travis, did she just say something dirty to you? Throw you off your game?" If Chris only knew.

"You know it, Chris. I mean wife dirty talk is at a whole new level." I replied, but I wasn't sure if anyone bought it. Now my imagination of what could be was within my grasp but it was no longer a simple exercise of what *could* be. Now we were getting into downright planning and organizing. There was, however, still a big chance that it was a false positive if I correctly remember. There's a reason people don't tell anyone

One Golden Day

before the third month. But I'm just not in a position to ask Leighton about this right now. I can't believe it. All the thoughts in my head had come to a stop with those two little words.

At that moment I heard someone screaming from the back of the restaurant. "Leighton, your dad can't breathe! Help, he can't breathe! Someone call 911."

In an instant, Leighton shot up, ran over to the table, got to her dad, checked his airways, noticed he was choking, and started the Heimlich maneuver.

"Everyone move back, give me some room. Dad I need you to try and take a big deep breath and let it all out."

As he tried to let the air out, she started to perform the maneuver, freeing the lodged food in his throat. As it projected across the table onto the floor, his purple face began to regain color.

"Dad, you should be okay, but I would still get checked out by an ambulance or at least an urgent care unit." Leighton was looking out for her dad, but I doubt he will.

"Leighton, I'll be fine. I'll have you keep an eye on me. I have you and your mother, which got me this far in life. What more do I need?"

He kind of had a point. Although he was a stubborn old ox

One Golden Day

of a man, he had made it this far being that stubborn old ox, so why stop now? Just keep doing what worked.

We asked around to see if anyone had called 911, and it looked like no one had. People had been waiting to see if Leighton herself would do, and the rest assumed that someone else had already made the call. It was a good thing Leighton was able to do the Heimlich properly and open her father's air passage, or who knows where or how he'd be right now.

"Dad, you need to get checked out, but as usual, you can be the old bull sitting in the field until you die, stubborn as can be. There's nothing we can do about it. Will you at least let me check your vitals every so often to make sure nothing major changes?"

"Not really, we're going to get going. I promised my buddies that I would still make it to poker, and it's getting late. You know I always play poker on Saturdays."

"Dad, you're leaving my wedding to go play poker with your friends, even after I saved your life?"

"I've been playing this game for almost ten years; you knew that when you planned your wedding. It's not my fault. Now I must get going. I love you, honey." Her dad was cold.

"Mom, you're just going to let him leave like this?" She just stared at Leighton, saying nothing.

As they left, Leighton looked at me with that distraught look in her eyes, not knowing what to do, how to take it. She didn't want to cry, not today, at our wedding. She wasn't going to let her parents ruin her day, not like this. As they grabbed their coats and started making their way out the door, she reached for my hand and held it tightly, then squeezed it and leaned into me.

"Lei, you going to be okay?"

"Yeah, the night was going well. I thought we might have a chance at building off this, but then this happened. At least I know I tried, and I can be okay with that."

She was such a tough one. She put her heart in and devoted it all and didn't hold back. Then if she got burned, she mended and went right back to it. It's that heart that has drawn me to her and keeps me falling for her over and over. She's just one amazing woman. Now there's a great chance I get to start a family with her, raise a child with her, and be a parent with her. I still can't believe this; we are going to get to be parents! It's hard to not want to scream it from the rafters, especially on our wedding night. Still, it would be horrible if something happened and we had to explain to people that Leighton lost

One Golden Day

the baby, or the test was a false positive.

"I love you, Lei. I always have your back and will support you no matter what. I wish I didn't have to watch you get hurt like this, but I understand it."

"Thanks, Travis, I love you too."

I grabbed her hand tight and pulled her off to the side so we could talk in private. Because everyone had just seen her father make a quick exit, no one thought anything of it. Though I was still lost a bit and in a haze, I was trying to do my best to show Leighton support and be there for her.

"I know that your dad is wrong, but can we talk about that bomb you just dropped on me back there: you're pregnant! I'm happy, just caught off guard."

"I know it's crazy right? I wanted to tell you, but wasn't certain. I took a pregnancy test today. Your mom is actually the one who bought it for me; she ran out and got one."

So that's where my mom had gone earlier in the day. Right before she left, I thought she'd run home to grab a basketball but it turned out that she was getting a pregnancy test for Leighton. I can't believe it, but I do understand that my mom kept this from me all day. It was crazy to think the women in my life had kept such a huge secret from me.

One Golden Day

"I love you, I'm so excited, and I can't wait to be a father! How far along would you think you are? Or do you even have any idea?"

Leighton leaned in, gave a big kiss and a long hug, we just sat there curled up thinking about everything quietly, then she eventually said to me. "I don't know, I just realized I missed my period last month, so I'm assuming it's super early. That's why I didn't want to say anything right away."

"I'm assuming we need to keep this quiet for a while until you get to your doctor and get checked up, to get a better understanding for sure how far along and if you really are pregnant?" "Yeah, it's not uncommon for those over-the-counter tests to give you a false positive, so to be safe, I want to see what the doctor says. I've got an appointment at the end of the week."

Leighton spent the next twenty minutes explaining to me the reason why we should wait. Not only because the doctor should check over the test she used but also how common it was for women to lose a pregnancy early on in the first trimester. I didn't even know that was an issue or possibility. That's nuts, to think so many pregnancies are lost. I guess it makes sense when you consider how many things need to go right for a

One Golden Day

pregnancy to stick.

"I get it, Lei. I'll be excited, hopeful, but measured until we can be certain."

"That's the best way. That way if anything happens, we can deal with it ourselves, and we don't have to go back through it explaining to everyone."

"I guess that makes sense, but it's so hard. I want to tell everyone like Terra just got to. But I also know she's halfway through the process. I guess it's different, huh?"

"Yes, it's different Travis, very different. She's halfway down the basketball court, and we're

barely putting on our shoes." I chuckled a bit.

"I get it, I'll have to do my best to stay collected and calm. Love you, Lei."

"Love you too, Travis."

As we made our way back into the room, I could see my mother was staring at me, given she was no doubt aware of everything that we had talked about. She made a beeline for me, and Leighton grabbed me by the hand.

"Leighton, is it okay if I take Travis for a quick walk around outside and talk to him for a bit? A little motherly talk to go over everything about Terra, and well, you know, your news?"

One Golden Day

"Yes, Mrs. Golden, you know that would be just fine. I'm going to go sit down and visit with Terra. I'll see you guys in a few."

Just like that, my mother and I turned around and walked out the front door. It was a nice cool summer night in Amarillo. We made our way around the plaza, just walking and talking and enjoying each other's company. We talked about the day, the craziness that had ensued, and how good it was to have Terra back home.

"Mom, what do you think about everything with Terra and Chis? I mean, if it was going to happen, I'm glad it's him because I know he's going to work his butt off to make it work and be there for Terra and their child together."

"I agree with you on that. Chris is one of a kind, and the way he loves Terra, the way he looked at her before she was carrying their child, is only amplified by that fact. The love he has for her is immeasurable. I'm excited to be a grandmother, to see what happens, and see what the future holds. Not to mention the news your bride dropped on you just a while ago. That is the main reason I wanted to walk with you."

"I'm okay, Mom, I know you're worried, but I'm okay."

"Travis, you are a really big planner; everything in your life

One Golden Day

going back to high school has been mapped out and organized. Nothing about being pregnant goes according to plan. It's more about waking up with a plan and throwing it out the window in the first fifteen minutes."

My mother spent the next fifteen minutes scaring me and reassuring me that we would be okay, but I that I have to be open to change, adapting, and growing. She said there is nothing like that moment you see your child for the first time. It just changes you; it's like a switch inside you is turned on. I've heard people talk about it, and they all explain it the same way—it's like Zeus himself struck them with a lightning bolt, charging them with the care of this child, waking up their inner superhero.

"Mom, I get it, you're scared and excited for me, but you also know I'm going to put the work
in to succeed at anything I do. I'm going to try and be the best dad I can be no matter what. I'm sure I'll make mistakes, but I'll learn and do better. That's all I can do and hope for."

"I know, Travis. I love you."

"Mom, I'll be honest, I'm a little worried about Terra and Chris. I know he will work his butt off to make it work. My biggest concern is whether or not she is humble enough to see he is an amazing man. I'm hoping she doesn't miss out on the things that most mothers get to be a part of with their kids because she is so driven. In other words, I fear she is going to go down dad's path, and not learn from it."

"I know, I'm a little worried too, but the biggest difference is when you're a dad you don't have to or get to carry the baby in your womb, like a mother does. It's a very hard thing to ignore that. There is a very strong bonding that goes on during those nine months. I can only hope she grows a strong bond like most mothers and develops that missing empathy we both feel she has missed as of late."

I know what you are thinking: Could Terra really be this disconnected from life right now? Did her cancer or that injury as a kid really mess her up this bad? The answer is, yes, it kind of did. She had a major injury that separated her from other kids during a very important developmental part of her life when she was younger. Then you add into it that she is a twin, and we twins have trouble bonding with others outside of that relationship because there is nothing quite like it. When you add up her life experiences, you realize the emotional drain it can put on someone that age. Mixed with our upbringing, then the cancer diagnosis and fight in her twenties, you get someone that eventually just shuts down. I hope, believe, and think she will pull through, but only Terra knows what is going on inside that mind and heart of hers.

One can only assume that going through the process of trying to save lives, with all her research, has taught her the value of her life and that of others. She has become so scientific, so black-and-white with everything, that's where the biggest issue come in. Chris is one big-ass teddy bear though, who adapts well to the world around him. His ability to support, love, and just be a driving force in Terra's and the baby's life will be huge for her. I just hope Terra doesn't push him away to the point that she ends up on the wrong side of the equation.

"Mom, I know she's been through a lot, but a part of growing up is recognizing it. I would assume, like you said, that going through this process will help with that. We all know Chris too; he's the perfect guy and support system for Terra while she's out there pulling double duty as world saver and mother."

"I hope so, believe so, and think she'll do great. I think this will bring her to another level even in her research, making it even more important than it already is. Babies have a way of driving you harder than ever before. Just ask your father," she said with a smile.

"What do you mean by that? I thought Dad was working for the state department already when you guys got married."

"Well, he was, but it was a lower-tiered job that didn't require much travel. We were actually living in Virginia at the time. We found out I was pregnant and wanted to really focus on starting a family. Around the same time, an opportunity came up that would allow his career to blossom, what you know of it today, but it was a big choice. We decided that I would move to Amarillo, and your father would travel out of Amarillo and Dallas but be home for two weeks every six weeks."

"Wait, so you knew he would be gone almost two months at a time, and you were okay with it?"

"Travis, look at how much you travel for your dream job in the NBA. Leighton knew going in that was your dream. Just like I knew going in that your father wanted to impact the world on a global scale, and he had a gift for it. It was one of the things I loved about him. And that comes with a price, a sacrifice."

"I guess that makes perfect sense when you explain it like that." My mom is good like that.

One Golden Day

Terra will be in good hands. I know I've said it, but Chris is the kind of person—like my mother, like Leighton—who knows what he's getting into. He will put in the work, sacrificing for the support of another. He knew when he got involved with Terra that her work would often be a top priority. Being as driven as she is can be what's also attractive about her. I'm sure that's what drew my mother, like she said, to my father, and Leighton to me. It's our drive—our internal push to do what others deem impossible.

14

Back Inside, Everyone Staring At Me

As we finished our lap around the parking lot, we kept talking about Terra. All the stories of how she had grown up involved so many of her as a kid watching her brother succeed in areas where she used to excel. She put in twice the effort in her studies as I did in basketball. I had natural talent, and both of us were gifted students. Still, Terra put in an exponential amount of extra work academically. She pushed herself, wanting to be the best at everything she could if it had a ranking, locally or the state level. You bet your ass she was studying for it until she passed out. Terra took academic competition to a whole different level then I ever took athletics.

We pushed each other, but I remember having conversations with her as a kid where I would have to walk her back and get her to calm down because she was so driven. I could see her getting physically worn out or worked up, so much so that I thought she might hurt someone. It was almost like watching a baseball pitcher get worked up on the mound when they feel like they're giving their best stuff. But it's just not working right and they get angry. The coach has to go out there and tell them that they can't start pegging batters because they're pissed.

Terra was a freshman in high school, and there was a state writing competition that started out locally. Then the top three local submissions from each school district were submitted to the state competition. Terra felt that the other two submissions from our school district were so poor that it might look poorly on hers too. Let me start off by saying she didn't think she was better than others or stuck up. She was just that competitive, that judgmental, when it came to competition—every single variable mattered.

"Travis, I'm telling you if the board reading this essay looks at them by school district, I'm screwed. They are going to look at them and think mine is only good because the other two are poor and penalize me," she said with a crazed look in her eyes.

"Terra, you're nuts. I know you want to win, and I know you worked your ass off on that piece, but you need to trust the work you put in. It's like the coach always says, 'You have to trust the work you put in to set yourself up for the best opportunity to win.' You know you put the work in. At this point it's subjective. You know the work you did was awesome, whether

you win or lose."

"Wait, now my own brother thinks I might lose? You're trying to prepare me for a loss." She was starting to hyperventilate.

"Calm down, Terra. Sit down, breathe slowly, and think it through. You don't know the judges; you don't even know if they're smart enough to understand the complexity of the piece you wrote, let alone the true meaning of Edgar Allen Poe's "The Raven." That got a chuckle.

"Travis, you're an idiot. Thank you, though, for calming me down. And you're right. For all, I know it's being graded by a gym teacher and someone who can barely read. I'm getting worked up about the other local submissions. I should be getting worked up about the idiots that are reviewing these things."

Here we go again; it took me nearly an hour to walk her back off the ledge of chaos. But that's what it's like with Terra. She's driven to succeed at all costs. She will think through as many variables as she can to overcome what she needs to overcome

One Golden Day

for a successful resolution.

"Hey Mom, do you remember that essay Terra came in second with when she was a freshman in high school when she almost lost her shit that whole week? We constantly had to walk her back."

"Travis, you mean the one where she did a little investigative journalism and found out the winner of the scholarship and the contest was none other than the niece of a judge? They ended up disbanding the whole thing and pressing charges. I wonder what came of all those involved."

"Terra was always one to get to the truth, which is what makes her an amazing researcher. She's like a bloodhound on a scent."

As we made our way back into the restaurant, it felt like everyone had their eyes on me. Then again, I could be in a state of paranoia from the news my wife dropped on me, Terra dropping in, and the walk my mother and I had just taken. I guess it could also simply be that I was the groom, my mother and I just took a twenty-minute walk, and my wife's parents just left the restaurant. They just straight-up dropped out, told her they had other shit to do. Her dad told her that his regular poker game was much more important than his daughter's wedding. That's got to be a rough one to take, so that might be why people are looking at me.

Leighton made her way over to me, grabbed me by the hand, then yanked me in hard as shit and damn near broke my hand.

"Come here, Travis Golden, you have some explaining to do." I was so lost at that moment. "Leighton, what are you talking about? How did I get in trouble for something when I was

outside walking with my mother?" Not being around has never stopped me from getting in trouble

before.

"What is this shit I heard that you and your groomsmen were drinking before the wedding?" "That's what this is about? It was like two drinks, and it was three for four hours before the wedding. By the time the ceremony started we hadn't had anything to drink for hours. What's the big deal? They had toasted me and the wedding. Hellm my mom even did a shot of tequila."

"You guys did shots of tequila?"

I should have quit while I was ahead. "Are you really this upset, or are you mad about your parents and taking this out on me a bit, because you can't yell at them right now? How many times did you call or text them since I went out to talk with my mom, and they didn't even bother to answer?"

"F-you Travis Golden, no one wants the truth thrown in their face on their wedding day."

Right then, she started to cry, leaned in, and put her face into my shoulder. All five foot seven feet of her fit perfectly into my shoulder. She cuddles up and snuggles in nice, even when she's mad at me. I know it wasn't the nicest thing to say, but when it comes to her parents, I've learned to rip the Band-Aid off, deal with the scream, and get through it. Otherwise, that shit lingers for days.

"Lei, you know I love you. You can talk shit to me, yell at me, and blame me all you want for the next couple days, but we both know who you're more pissed at right now."

"I know. I just don't get it. Who the hell does that?"

She had a point, but as I've pointed out, her parents had a history of this. I remember our first Christmas; we had only been dating about two months when I found out her parents had decided to go out of town before she got home from school. They weren't coming back until after New Year's. She had waited until a few days before Christmas to come home, only to find out her parents had decided to go to Vegas for the holidays, without her. Like I said, they liked to remind her that she was old enough to take care of herself from the time she was in middle school.

"Do you remember our first Christmas together, Lei? Remember all that shit you had to deal with? How embarrassed you felt spending the holidays with us? But eventually, it all melted away. You relaxed and remembered we don't get to pick our parents or our family. Still, we do get to choose who we allow in. We get to choose who we associate with, who we treat like family, who we bring in close. You taught me that."

"I know Travis, and it's easier said than done some days, especially on days like today, when you want your dad to walk you down the aisle and act like he cares, just for a moment. Truth be told, I wanted your dad here just as much as you. Because they have been as impactful in my life as yours. The way they have opened their home to me—not just as your girlfriend, fiancee, or wife, but as simple caring people? That have taught me what it's like to be loved. Not just by you, but by parental influence. I don't know what I'd do without them, without you."

"I know, Lei. We aren't perfect, but we are loving and

always seem to show up when it truly matters. Terra is the prime example of that. She's been off trying to save the world for a year, and she found a way to make it here."

"That's what I love about your family, Travis. You guys always show up. It may not be on time, it may be a little late, but you will make up for any lost time and show someone you truly support them. It's something I've missed for so long."

"Are you saying you wanted to marry my family just as much as you wanted to marry me?" I said jokingly, trying to lighten the mood.

"Travis, can we be serious for a minute? Come on, you know I love your crazy ass. Hell, I followed you to New Orleans."

"You love New Orleans first of all, so don't give me that shit. Well, we both do."

As the two of us were going back and forth reminiscing about our Christmas holidays, I noticed that Chris and Terra were off in a corner planning, judging by the fact that she was holding a pen and writing something out. My mother was sitting next to them talking with my father but trying her hardest to listen in on everything Terra and Chris were saying. Most of our friends and family were starting to work their way

One Golden Day

out the door at this point. We had gone from the wedding to the reception, had a choking hazard, watched my wife's father leave for his weekly poker game with the guys, get surprised by my father showing up at the wedding, and my sister showing up pregnant, carrying my best friend's baby. I'd say it had been a pretty memorable wedding.

"Hey Lei, calm down. Just slow down. Can we just sit down and relax for a minute? I just want to sit here and enjoy it."
"Yes, we can just sit here. Is everything okay? Or are you just taking Father Dan's advice?" "Exactly, just taking some great advice from a great guy."
As we sat down, held hands, and just sat there, Father Dan walked over. "Do you guys mind if I sit here quietly with you?"
"By all means, have at it. Take a seat."
It was nice; it almost felt like a commercial for a beer: when they take the top off a beer, and you're whisked away to an island vacation to enjoy life somewhere else. A calmness came over me. I could feel Leighton's shoulders finally relax after watching her be so tense for so long. Father Dan slouched back in his chair, sipped on his gin, and we all sat there quietly, enjoying the evening—what had been, what was, and what might come of it. As Father Dan was staying in Cincinnati at the moment,

One Golden Day

we'd had to fly him in and put him up. Instead of putting him in a hotel, my parents wanted to put him up in their house so they could visit with him more often. I know Leighton, and I had a hotel room reserved for the night, but something told me that, with my dad home, Terra home, and Father Dan here, we were going to end up back at the house with a big-ass sleepover.

"Hey, where are you two kids staying tonight? Did you get a hotel?" Father Dan was fishing. "We did get a hotel downtown, but I think we'll end up coming back to the house for a bit to visit, especially with Terra in town." Leighton jumped in, saving me the question.

"With the night winding down, I was about to grab Mom and Dad, and get the family wound up and get some rides organized. Did anyone see where Chris went with Colleen? I saw them leave a few minutes ago." I honestly was confused.

"Travis, they went to go get our car for us. Colleen drove here and was nice enough to drive Terra and Chris over to the church to get your car and his car, so they can bring them back to the restaurant."

"Wait. Is Chris sober enough to drive? I'll be honest. I didn't see him drink much all night, or anyone else for that matter. Just wondering." I didn't see anyone else drinking, other than her dad that is. "He's fine, no one really drank as expected, but we probably all will when we go back to your parents' house."

"On that note, I'll go grab my pops and start closing up shop, get organized, and see what is left to be done."

I made my way over to my parents, looking for anything and everything I could grab to start cleaning up and organizing. I wanted to minimize steps and maximize efficiency because the quicker we could get ready, the faster we could get back to the house, which is where the real party would happen.

It would only be a few of us, but that's where the best stories, the fun, and the family shenanigans would ensue. That house had so many memories—it's where we'd grown up, learned to ride bikes, where I'd learned to shoot the perfect jump shot, and where I had my first kiss (don't tell Leighton!).

The house is on a street called Lipscomb in Amarillo, one of the oldest streets and neighborhoods in town. The neighborhood is called Wolflin Historic. I remember growing up when we told people we lived there they would often roll their eyes, and say, how nice. But what they didn't know was the work my parents put into that house. It was built back in the forties, had tons of history, but that also meant lots of work needed to be done on it. They even told us a story of how the house didn't even have a kitchen countertop in the kitchen when they bought it. That's one of the reasons the house sat there for so long. Mortgage companies wouldn't approve a loan without a countertop, and homeowners would install a kitchen counter, so it became a stalemate between seller and buyer.

The house was a two-story house with a huge basement. For Texas, especially West Texas, having a basement was a luxury. To us, it was normal. However, the closest closet to my parents' bedroom was in the basement. They had a private staircase from their master bathroom to it. It led to a hallway where the laundry was, eventually leading to a media room my father built. Off of that was a huge dining room with a bar that my parents used for entertaining. The main floor featured a big office, a master bedroom and kitchen, a living room, and a dining room. There was the upstairs where Terra and I spent most of our days playing, getting in trouble, and causing a ruckus.

"Hey, Dad, are you guys getting ready to head back to the house and bring Farther Dan with you? Leighton said Colleen and Chris already went to get our cars so we can head that way shortly. I think I see them pulling up now."

"Yeah, they are closing us out. We'll be able to head out in a few minutes. Do you guys want any food? I've got them packing up a little bit of everything into one of the coolers I brought so we can load it up and bring it back to the house."

My dad loves this restaurant's cooking, and it is some of the best Italian food in Amarillo, probably all of West Texas. With all his traveling, he likes to fill up when he's in town. Even though he's around more, he still travels. I think last year alone he put over forty thousand miles on his car. He's also the leftovers guy in our family. He will not let any food go to waste. Mom says it's from all the war-torn countries he's seen over the years. When he goes to places that have no food, he can't handle any waste.

"I guess I'll grab Leighton, you grab Mom and Father Dan, and we'll meet you back at the house in a few? We're going to swing by the hotel first, check in, and change. We need to get into some casual clothes."

"Sounds like a plan son, take your time. I'm sure we'll be up late talking and visiting, especially with Terra in town."

After a long day at the church and a crazy day at the restaurant, it was time to grab my wife. That's right, she was my wife now. No longer my fiancée or girlfriend—and it feels great to say that. We could go back to our hotel, relax a little bit, and get comfortable. Then we would head over to the house and visit with friends and family. This would be the best part of the day where we would bring everyone together. Like Father Dan said, take time and enjoy it.

"Hey Leighton, I see Chris brought the car back. Did he and Terra already head over to the house?"

"Yeah, they did. She needs to put her feet up and change into something more comfortable, which is what we need to do. I can't wait to get out of this dress and put on something that's a bit more casual."

"I'll settle for just you out of the dress, but now that I know you're pregnant, I'm not sure I'm in the mood anymore. I just keep looking at you differently, like you're some priceless, fragile vase that I don't want to risk breaking."

"Two things: you'll get past that real quick in the hotel room once I get out of this dress, and second, you're too sweet." She's right, I am a pushover.

The crazy thing is, between the two of us, she has a healthier sexual appetite than I do. We never had a crazy sexy life when we were dating, which is probably from how we met and me

One Golden Day

always at the basketball facility in the college. But Leighton was usually the one working to grab my attention and get me in bed. It's not because she isn't sexy as hell, I'm just a wanderer, focused on other things—my mind wanders to so many different things. Leighton has always been the one that keeps me centered in life. Without her, I would be in a basketball gym nonstop, and I'd only leave to shower and sleep; I'd probably eat in the gym if I could.

"Lei you ready to head out? Let's say goodbye to everyone and go. We'll see them all shortly at the house, anyway."

"I already said goodbye, so we can head out. Your mom and dad are right behind us, and pretty much everyone else is outside already." As usual, Leighton was one step ahead and planning accordingly.

We made our way outside, hopped in the rental car, and drove downtown to our hotel. The ride was a short one from the restaurant: just a quick jaunt up Bell Street then I-40. But we just sat there quietly and didn't even talk. It was nice and to get away from the throng of people we'd been around all day and just sit in the car with Leighton. Hearing the hum of the road as we pulled into the hotel Leighton shot me a loaded look, reminding me it was our wedding night.

One Golden Day

15

Are We Going to Make It To the House?

When we checked into the room, I realized we had way too *much* room—booking the presidential suite was overkill. This was especially true given that, with Terra in town, we were going to be spending a ton of time at the house. We had overpacked and had way too much stuff. The room was huge, but it did feel nice to be able to afford it. Things were rough for Leighton growing up, and I like to give her the best in life when I can. I know I can't always go big, and spending too much can drive hernuts, but treating her like a queen is my job.

"Travis, I know you like spoiling me, and you like spoiling us time and again, but this room is huge. We don't need it," she told me.

I know.

"If they had something in between this room and the other

One Golden Day

rooms, I would have gotten it, but they didn't, so this is what we got. It's our wedding night, and you just married an NBA player who recently signed a new NBA contract. It's even guaranteed for five more years. So we are going to splurge a bit on a hotel in Amarillo."

"Okay, fair enough, I guess you have a point there. Seeing as we only have so much time before we should head over, can you help me out of this dress?"

"You know I can." As I started to unzip her dress she turned to me, and we started kissing and disappeared into the moment. We have had plenty of nights together, crazy dumb hookups in places I'm not going to bring up in case my parents are reading this. But tonight was different. I just got lost in her. We just fell into the love song that had been connecting us all these years. It was almost like living your favorite love song—the emotion and goose bumps it gives you. Every thought it brought up was lived in that hour. We laughed, kissed, played around, and enjoyed each other's bodies in a way I've never done with anyone before. It wasn't about the physical, but it rarely was with Leighton and me. Still, tonight was different, with so many emotions from the day. It was a culmination and release of the good *and* the bad.

One Golden Day

"I guess I got you out of your dress and then some? Did you enjoy your massage? I can't remember the last time I gave you a massage like that."

"You mean longer than three minutes? I'd say not since the first couple weeks we were dating when you were trying to get in my pants, Travis Golden." Leighton was laughing and smiling.

"Fair enough, that was my college move, but it landed me the best girl at Texas Tech. I'd say it worked," I said, grinning.

"Alright Travis Golden, flattery will work. We should get a move on; everyone is going to be talking. Then again, they might give us some shit if we didn't take our time."

"Exactly. Let's get dressed and head over, but not before one more round."

I grabbed her, and we started tickling, kissing, and rolling around. One thing led to another, and we were back lost in that moment. I finally understood what those soul singers were singing about—the Teddy Pendergrasses of the world who my mother and father would listen to when I was younger. I remember one song vividly; it seems to be running through my head on a constant loop right now. It's a song by **one of my mother's favorite artists, Maxwell call "A Woman's Work.**

One Golden Day

[AU: Please reword this for clarity] If you've never heard the song, I suggest you light some candles, pour some wine, and treat your significant other to a night they deserve. I know it may seem odd to have a song my mom played in my head, but the words were finally ringing true and the emotion was hitting me right in my spine.

Leighton lay there smiling up at me; I couldn't take my eyes off her. I was rubbing her belly, wondering what might be and what our conversations might be like in a few weeks, a few months, or a year. There were so many variables up in the air, so many possibilities; just the mere possibility of new life had Leighton and me glowing.

"What are you thinking about, Travis? You always have that lost-in-the-distance gaze when you're lost in thought." She had that right; I get the same look at the free-throw line sometimes.

"Just wondering what might be and where we might end up with news about you being pregnant and all. I'm excited, ready for a new challenge, ready to start a family with you. I mean I know we have no clue what we're doing, but who does? That's fun. All I know is I want to figure it out together with you."

One Golden Day

"I'm right there with you babe. As long as we're in this chaos together I know we'll get through it. But I am concerned. I don't want to get my hopes up, but at the same point, it's really hard not to."

"Have you let yourself think about if you want a girl or a boy, or what names you might like? I know you just found out today. I'm just trying to gauge how far into this you've thought. I'll be happy either way. I just want you and the baby to be healthy, end of story." "Awe thanks, Travis. I'm not concerned about the sex either, I just want to us to be healthy too. As for names, no, but we're in New Orleans now, and we have some good strong family names, so we'll have plenty of ideas. We should probably get moving, by the way."

"I really don't want to, but we should."

We hopped up, did our fire drill on getting ready, jetted out of the hotel to the car, and sped over to the house. My parents' house isn't far from downtown, so it was a simple five-minute drive. As we pulled up, I could see my parents' coonhound mix in the window going nuts. She wasn't a puppy anymore but still young enough to be hyper. She goes friggin crazy when you come to the door, but eventually calms down after a few minutes. She's a great dog. She's pretty big too, probably eighty

One Golden Day

or so pounds.

We got to the house around nine-thirty, which for a wedding and reception you would think isn't very late, especially after all of the fireworks we'd had that day. It would be nice to sit around the house and just visit. I wondered if the neighbors would swing by. We invited them, but they both had to work and couldn't get the time off. They were doctors on call that weekend but got off around nine I think they said. Leighton knows better than me. In the house, my dad already had a round of mojitos for all of us ready to go. My mom pulled Leighton aside, giving her one that was mainly sprite and mint. It was nonalcoholic.

"Hey, Terra, come here. I didn't get to visit with you enough when we were at the restaurant.

Can I get a hug and some one on one time with my Sis?" I gave her the puppy dog look.

"I guess I did crash your wedding without confirming and dropped the news that I'm pregnant with your best friend's baby. Does that mean I owe you one?"

Chris stuck his head up from the table, where they were playing cards, "You talking 'bout me?"

"Just talking about our prowess as a baby maker, honey." I

One Golden Day

didn't need to hear that. "Thanks, Sis. Not sure I needed those words uttered aloud."

"Fair enough. What can our Sis do for her brother? By the way, I've still kept track of you and your stats; been watching your games too. Your jumper has been lagging. Have you had back tightness or a leg injury? I noticed you looked sluggish at the end of last season."

Terra could always spot a hip in my giddyap, even going back to when we were kids. If I had a growth spurt, she'd notice my shot change; she doesn't miss much. That's what makes her so amazing in her field; she catches all the small details.

"As usual, Sis, you noticed that my back got really tight toward the end of the season from a little too much stress and long season catching up. I need to get a new routine to ensure it doesn't happen this year. I started doing yoga in the offseason with Leighton. It's been great."

"That's good. Did your team doctor do a nutrition panel workup with your blood? My guess is that your diet has changed drastically over the past couple of years, with you moving to New Orleans, and you haven't noticed. But you decreased certain meats, getting more fats, and whatnot."

"I have been eating way more fish than ever, especially during

One Golden Day

crawfish season."

"Travis, that could increase your iron, magnesium, and so many other nutrients, causing muscle tightness and removing water from your muscles, minimizing elasticity. With a big move like that, especially going from a higher altitude to a lower altitude, so many factors have to be considered. I suggest finding a good dietitian and getting your blood checked regularly. Also, congrats on the new contract. Chris filled me in a little bit, that's awesome. If you ride it out, like I know you will, it'll be eight years in New Orleans. Well done."

"That's the goal, Sis, you never know. That's why we wanted it to be a team-friendly deal. I love the city, the team, and the owners, and I've wanted to play there my whole career. I know I'm not going to be the next superstar. I know my place, but I can make a big impact just the same."

"Don't sell yourself so short, Travis. I've watched plenty of games that the Pelicans wouldn't have won without the defense you played or the fifteen to twenty you also dropped in. You may not be a superstar, but you're one year away from being an established veteran. And you'll probably make it ten plus years in the league. You should be proud, Bro. I know I am."

"Enough about me, Sis. Can I ask you the burning question

One Golden Day

that I know Mom didn't ask you? I'm sure Chris didn't because he's too nice. Why didn't you tell anyone when you were pregnant and overseas? I get being a bit embarrassed, but what took so long to tell *us*?"

"To be honest, Travis, I just found out a few weeks ago. I kept putting weight on and went to the doctor. When they did a blood panel, they noticed something didn't look right, so they had me do a pregnancy check, and, well, you know the rest. With my condition and all the meds, I didn't think it was possible and turns out it was. I wasn't hiding anything, just trying to figure it all out."

"I guess it makes for a stressful trip, wondering what to say and how to say it, not to mention how long of a flight it was. Seriously, though how long of a flight?"

"Well, it was about nine hours from Paris to New York then another four hours to Dallas, then
the flight to Amarillo, so it took me a while to get here. But it was well worth it, more importantly, much needed. How are you and Leighton doing in New Orleans?"

"The usual, but Leighton has been growing the clinics with the help of the Pelicans' team owners and organization. It's been awesome to watch her grow it. Even cooler to watch is the impact she's had in communities with the kids."

One of the best parts of watching Leighton grow the clinic program is the impact it's had on the kids in the city. With them getting better healthcare, being healthy at school, they are getting better grades. Some of their test grades are improving overall too. It wasn't anything she originally had planned. Still, when she saw the impact, she started working with the team's local impact programs to help support tutoring programs in conjunction with the health clinics.

After Terra and I were finished catching up, we realized we were the only ones on the first floor. Apparently, everyone else had gone downstairs to hang out and talk. It's funny though that everyone just left Terra and me up here to visit. On second thought, it doesn't surprise me; it's something our family has been doing to us for some time.

There was one summer when we were on vacation in high school, and my parents left the two of us at home all day. We were thirteen at the time. They left us in the condo all day, went out, toured the island we were on, and we didn't even notice they were gone. Terra and I can be like that. If we get on a roll, we kind of get in a time warp and the world around us disappears. It's a twin thing. When we were in college, we met

One Golden Day

another set of twins who said they do the same thing. "Since everyone's ditched us, again, want to head downstairs and visit a little bit more, seeing as it's your wedding day and all, Bro?"

"You're the one who's pregnant, Sis. We have plenty to talk about and celebrate."

"That's one way of putting it. Speaking of events, how is Leighton after that scene with her parents earlier? I know the word *parents* is a little loose, but it can't make it any easier."

"She's doing okay, but it's still rough."

"I'll make sure and tread lightly with Leighton; the last thing I want to do is cause more of a stir than I already have on your wedding day."

We made our way downstairs. As we turned the corner at the bottom of the stairs into the room, everyone greeted us with a cheer and the sarcasm was duly noted. The room was pretty large in size, with a dining table big enough to seat ten. There was a wet bar in the corner and a random old leather loveseat in the corner. We'd thrown it there one day, thinking we'd move it a few days later. That was ten years ago.

"Hey, if it isn't the twins! I've heard stories about you two zoning out to the world around you,

but *that* was wild. I've never seen anything like it." Father Dan was giving us crap.

"I know we can get tied up in what we're talking about, but it can't be that bad."

"Just in case you didn't think it was, I had Leighton take a video of you two," my mom chimed in.

Just then Leighton pulled out her phone and showed us a video of Father Dan doing different things to try and get out attention, but we didn't even break. He walked up and said "Hey," clapped his hands at one point, and even dropped a book, but we just kept on talking. When Terra and I lock in on each other, the rest dissipates. That's why it sucked to not have her in my life this past year.

There were a lot of nights that I couldn't sleep. I would toss and turn, waking up from nightmares wondering what she was doing, how she was. I couldn't deal with not talking to her.

It really gave me anxiety that slowly fixated in my muscles, causing tension in my back and my hamstrings. I remember talking with the trainers about it, trying to come up with a new way to clear my mind, but I still couldn't find the right routine that didn't involve talking to her.

It was a rough period for sure in my life. Like I said, being a twin is about a connection unlike any other. Having that kind of connection with someone can be amazing when you have it, but also detrimental when you lose it. I know Terra was hiding in her work, burying herself in her research. The hard part for me was that she made the decision, it was her conscious choice, and she left me out of it. I was in the dark about why suddenly we'd stopped talking. It took me back a little bit when she told me she was still watching and keeping track of me, and had even noticed I was struggling with my health. If she noticed all those things, I don't know why she wouldn't have reached out. It's more reason to be worried about what this cancer did to her.

"Okay, we get it. We can disappear into twin land when we get talking. In our defense this time it's been a while since we've talked. I blame Terra, though, for all of that. Just saying." Here comes a punch.

"Hey, Bro, I was a little busy and dealing with some shit; lay off me. Sorry that my cancer was an inconvenience to you."

As she hit me, though she was a bit sarcastic, there was some semblance of truth in her words. It wasn't my place to be upset. Although we are all inherently selfish, we take things to heart even when we know we shouldn't.

"I get it, that comment was in poor taste. I'm sorry, Sis. But

One Golden Day

you know it hurt me too. I love you and missed the shit out of you. Now, enough sad shit, we have way too much to celebrate today. Who's up for some games?"

Just like that, we were off and running. It started off with a few family favorites that began with Terra's favorite dry-erase board, a little bit of family Pictionary. We are lazy or creative; it just depends on how you look at it. When playing the game, each person gets to write down four things they want. Then we put those in a bowl and draw randomly until we're done. It's how we've always played. We never used real games or boards. If we couldn't use a regular deck of fifty-two cards or something like that dry-erase board, we didn't play it.

"I guess I'll start. I'll pull first." I was prepared to be the sacrificial lamb. "Who the hell wrote *nursery*?" This was going to be a fun one. I planned to have a little fun at everyone else's expense and play dumb. I was going to start drawing baby plants all over this thing—that kind of a nursery, hah!

One Golden Day

16

It's Amazing How Many Game Nights End the Same Way

After an hour or so of people laughing, arguing, and making fun of each other during Pictionary, we decided to play a euchre tournament. The only downside is that it's hard to have a tournament when you only have three teams. What started as a great idea quickly ended when we realized there weren't that many teams.

"All right, so I guess it getting late and game night is starting to wind down. Time to throw on the TV, make some popcorn in the old popcorn maker, and watch a movie down here?" Dad had a good idea.

"My only concern is when was the last time you cleaned that old popcorn maker?" Terra said.

"Yeah, Mr. Golden, last time Travis and I were in town it looked pretty rough." Leighton also piled on.

One Golden Day

"I'll have you all know I cleaned it the other day, and even ran it through the dishwasher preparing for tonight, even though I'm a firm believer that dirty, oily popcorn machines make better popcorn."

Dad had a good point; we don't question the nastiness at the movie theater. But here we were giving him the business about his movie-style popcorn maker. It made damn good popcorn though, so maybe it *was* all about the built-up oil and grease. One thing was for sure. We were about to find out if cleaning it would make the popcorn better or worse.

"Dad, did you already start making some? I can smell it, the oil, salt, and that distinct smell in the basement brings me back to being a kid." Terra sat there with a big smile on her face.

"I can't go that far back, but it does remind me of my first Christmas in this house with you guys. I know we've talked about it a little bit tonight, Travis, but smelling that fresh smell makes me think of warm pj's and Christmas movies here." Leighton was hit with that nostalgia whiff.

You could see everyone in the room was also hit with the idea of a back-in-the-day syndrome. It really does remind me of the good old days. I was with Leighton a little bit, then again it was my wedding day, so sitting there thinking of our first holiday

One Golden Day

together seemed about right.

We'd been barely dating when I reached out to her to see how her day had been going.

One Golden Day

"Hey, Leighton, so how's it being back home for break? You guys have anything special going on?" I had asked her over the phone.

"Nothing major. We don't have a lot of family, so it's just going to be a lot of lounging around and being lazy for a week, then back to school. You?"

"We don't have a ton of family either, but what we do have is plenty of tradition and fun. You should come over one day, or for a few of them. My mom goes all-out over the holidays."

"I'll have to see what time I have free, but we'll figure it out," she said, seeming almost sad.

"Didn't you just say you aren't doing much? Come on, it'll be fun I promise. Well, we're here, I'm here. Text me. I'll give you the address. You're free to stop any time," I told her.

"Thanks, Travis. That's very nice of you, but I'll have to see what my parents are doing. I've got to go; I'll talk to you later."

That was odd; normally it was hard to get Leighton off the phone. Then again, people can always act differently around their family. I decided I'd give her a little time, then text her and see how she was doing.

I then spent a good hour or so doing stuff around the house for my mom—cleaning up, running errands, doing the usual home-for-the-holiday's strong young son stuff. You know what I'm talking about: moving heavy shit around the yard and randomly moving furniture so she could clean behind it—stuff like that. I finally took a break to sit down, grab some water, chill on the couch, and text Leighton.

"Hey, Leighton, is your day any better? You seemed down earlier."

"It's not great, but thanks for checking on me. What are you doing?"

"Moving heavy things for my mom most of the day. You?"

"Eh, I changed my mind. I think I'll come over if the invite is still open."

"Always. Come over in like two hours?"

"Sounds good. Dress anything special?"

"Well, you'll be meeting my parents, so I'd take that into account, but don't dress for the prom, LOL."

"Travis, you're an idiot. I'll see you in a bit."

"Bye, Leighton."

Just like that, I had to inform my mom that I had a serious girlfriend and that she was coming over in a few hours to visit. My mom wasn't keen on surprises. Then again, who of us is unless it is something for us, like a gift. This was going to be a fun conversation but I needed Mom to meet Leighton without Terra being around. If Terra was in the room, she would just antagonize Mom and get her riled up.

Mom and Terra were working on decorations in the main room, going through ornaments, tinsel, and all the cheery holiday stuff.

"Hey, Mom, do you have a second to talk to me?"

"Sure, honey, what is it? We're just going through all this stuff, getting it organized."

"Yeah, Bro, your break is over. You should either sit and help or start moving more boxes up here." Terra was a bit feisty, which was not good.

"Mom, I was kind of hoping to talk to you in private. I mean, it's okay, it can wait." But it really couldn't.

"Travis, what's up? Is everything okay, are you okay?" Mom looked really confused and I didn't blame her.

"Yeah, it's fine, I just need to tell you something, I just...never mind."

"Sounds like Travis doesn't want me around. I can leave Bro," Terra said.

"No, Sis, that's not it at all. I just wanted to tell mom that I

One Golden Day

have a girlfriend of almost three months from college, who lives in Amarillo, and she's coming over in a little bit, that's all."

"Wait. For what, Bro? You have a girlfriend, and you haven't told anyone, not even me? Mom, this is some serious stuff, time to dig." This is what I was afraid of.

"Terra, give your brother a break. Travis, she has a point, why didn't you tell anyone? And I guess we need to clean the house up a bit before we have a guest over."

"I wasn't going to invite her, but she sounded really down. I wasn't sure what it was, so I thought being around us, even if just relaxing, would be better than being sad."

I can't believe those words had just come out of my mouth. Could I be falling for a girl, seriously falling for a girl already? It's not like me. I've always been focused on my goals, hoops especially, but there's something about this girl, not sure what it is, but there's something there.

After two hours of scrambling to get decorations up, cleaning the house, and getting ready, Leighton messaged she was on her way. When she arrived at the front door, I felt nervous, like it was our first date all over again.

"She's here; don't be too crazy, Terra." Wait, did I just say that?

One Golden Day

"Travis has it bad for this one. I've never seen him like this. Then again he's never invited a girl over. This is going to be fun." Terra was relishing it.

"Both of you behave. Terra, don't give him too hard of a time." Thanks, Mom.

As I opened the door, I could see Leighton on the front stoop. She was shy, and was almost curled up in a ball while standing, trying to hide in plain sight on our doorstep. It was so cute; it was like watching a cat trying to curl up in a ball.

"Come on in, Leighton, thanks for coming over, too. I'm glad you decided to."

"Me too, I needed to get out of that house. By the way, you failed to mention you grew up in Wolfin, let alone Wolflin Historic. Your house and neighborhood are gorgeous."

"Compared to the houses up the block we're roughing it. I guess it's all perspective, but I get it. Come on it, we don't need to stand in the doorway the whole time. This is my twin sister, Terra."

"Whoa, you two are spitting images, but can I say she is way prettier than you are handsome, and I think you're sexy Travis, just saying."

"Thank you, Leighton, flattery will get you everywhere with

One Golden Day

me." Nice one, Leighton.

"This must be your mom, the woman I get to thank for raising such a gentleman. Your son really has been one of the few nice guys on campus."

"Why thank you, Leighton, he is a pretty good kid. His grandmother and I kicked his butt a bit." Yeah, they did.

"Why don't we give you a quick tour of the house, while Travis helps finish up a few things with his dad outside? We can do a little girl talk."

"This can't be good. Then again, I did invite you over. You're in good hands." It was just at the moment they walked away that I heard my sister ask, "So how did you two meet?"

Leighton looked at me with a level of fear that should be saved for only war time. It was like, "Holy shit, what am I supposed to do? We met because I threw up all over you, Travis. Save me." So I stepped up to save the day.

"We met when I was bartending at Hoots. She and some friends came in. She left her ID, and came back the next day when it was slower. We talked and hit it off."

She looked at me like, "Thank you, let's see how long we can keep this up," which was a good point because if we dated a long time, it would eventually come out. The crazy thing is

One Golden Day

we've been able to keep it quiet for a long time. That's the kind of guy Chris is. He wasn't going to run around saying stuff he shouldn't. And he's the only other person who knows about my relationship with Leighton, because he was there that night.

After a good hour or so finishing up stuff with my dad, we walked inside to find that the girl was sitting there eating pizza and having a good time. At least—they were having a good time for the time being. That's when it was all about to change. "Hey, were you going to tell Dad and me that you had pizza here?" I asked Terra.

"Hell, no. Once *you* got in here, it would all be gone." Terra was right; I can smash a whole pizza easily.

"Thanks for inviting me over, Travis. It's been great getting to know your mom and sister. It's easy to see how you turned out the way you did with these two on you."

"Yeah, and don't forget Grandma until she passed. I've always had strong women kicking my butt."

"Hey Leighton, all this talk of us. What about your family, your parents? What are you guys doing for the holidays? Any traditions?" Terra started digging.

"Nothing major, holidays and my family don't mix well. It's like any other day usually."

One Golden Day

"That sucks, Leighton. Are your parents just busy working? Are they doctors or something, or just not into holidays?" Terra kept at it.

"Honestly, I don't have the greatest parents. And I'd rather not talk about it unless you have a bottle of wine or two lying around and a few hours." As she started fighting back the tears, I leaned in.

"Terra, calm down and lay off her. Obviously, her parents are a touchy subject. Can you let it go? It's okay Leighton. I'm sorry."

Just like that, Terra got up, walked away, and went into the kitchen.

"It's okay, Terra didn't know, she was just asking about my family. It's not her fault. My parents are useless assholes. Pardon my language, they LEFT ME ALONE FOR CHRISTMAS WITHOUT TELLING ME!!" Now came the tears. "That's why you were down all day. Why didn't you say something and come over sooner?
Leighton, that's bullshit, come here." I gave her the biggest hug and just let her cry it out.

My mom got up and gave us some privacy for a few moments, then she came back in after she heard us quiet down and get back a talking tone.

"This isn't something I normally do, but you are both in college, and you shouldn't be spending the holidays home alone, that's not cool. We have plenty of room here and a guest room. After talking to Mr. Golden and Terra, we'd love to invite you to stay with us the rest of your break. If it's okay with Travis, we are happy to give you the Christmas of family fun you never had."

"Are you serious, Mrs. Golden? I couldn't impose on you guys and your generosity; I feel bad enough already." She was still fighting back the tears—and even some hiccups at this point.

"Leighton, it's okay, my family is just this nice. We have big hearts. Oh, we can get on each other's nerves and drive each other crazy, but we show up when it matters. Right now, it matters. You should hang for the week. Come on, it'll be fun."

"Leighton, come on. I promise it'll be a good time, not to mention we'll feel really bad if we know you're sleeping in an empty place over the holidays. For our own selfishness, hang here." Terra has a different way of saying nice things sometimes.

Fighting back a bit of a chuckle Leighton managed to say,

One Golden Day

"Okay, I'll stay. Travis can you come with me to grab my stuff then? I don't have a ton; I travel light."

"You know it, girl. Let's grab some food, relax a bit, then we can go grab your stuff."

That's how we found out about Leighton's shit parents, and I'm pretty sure that's when my relationship with her went from infatuation and fun to deeper affection and—dare, I say it, love. I mean, you already know we ended up getting married, so I spoiled the lead on that one.

17

I'm Telling You, Die Hard *Is a Christmas Movie*

Now here we all were, sitting in the basement around a table, with the smell of popcorn filling the air. It took me back to that fateful day when Leighton had come over to share the Christmas holiday with us. I remember sitting there, watching my dad's favorite Christmas movie, which I know is up for debate. Still, it's a tradition to kick off the break with his favorite. (My mom isn't a fan of watching *Die Hard* and calling it a Christmas movie.)

The subject came up again. Seems my dad just couldn't leave it alone.

"Father Dan is a man of the cloth. He has God's ear, and even He knows that *Die Hard* is a Christmas movie. Isn't that correct, sir?" Dad looked at his friend for support.

"I'm not sure I'm going to bring the big guy in on this

debate, but I will say I think it's a Christmas movie, straight up and down, no argument." Father Dan had spoken.

"Every year we have this argument, every freaking year. It's *not* a Christmas movie. If there's a movie and there's a baby in it, that doesn't make the movie a baby movie any more than *Die Hard* is a Christmas movie." Mom was making her point as usual but Terra had guns loaded.

"I agree with Mom, but I'm starting to come around on this one as I get older. I think it's closer to a Christmas movie than not. I'm not saying you can put it on par with *Miracle on 34th Street,* but it's still a Christmas movie." Wow, I didn't see that one coming.

"What do Leighton and Chris think of this, as the outsiders of the group?" Father Dan interjected.

"They have stayed out of it as long as I've known both of them. They're not willing to commit to either one. Chris will tell you he's not a fan one way or another of the movie, and I think Leighton learned from him to say the same thing somehow. They are like Switzerland. They play no sides, they just sit in the middle."

"Hey, I resent that, even if it is a bit true," Chris chimed in with a smile and a "Cheers" look that would ace an audition for a beer commercial.

"I'm just noncommittal on family feuds that aren't mine in general, especially ones about movies," Leighton said, smiling.

"See, just like the Swiss, won't commit to anything, playing the neutral party. No popcorn for them unless they choose a side. There must be a consequence." Okay, so I might have been going a

bit overboard.

It was Mom's turn to weigh in again. "Are we really having a debate over this right now? Every year we bring this up. I thought we had an agreement to drop the debate as to whether or not we could watch it every year?"

"I'm just saying it's an age-old question: is *Die Hard* the greatest Christmas movie of all time? It's definitely packed with the most action."

"Well said, Dad," I told him. But maybe I should shut up.

"Here, Here!" Father Dan raised his glass.

This really went on for a good twenty or so as we rustled and piled into a room that wasn't much larger than a bedroom. And yet it had been turned into a cozy media room. You couldn't call it a movie room, because it wasn't big enough. At least that's what we told my Dad, just to give him a hard time.

One Golden Day

As everyone was piling in, Leighton and I fell back a little bit and had one more of those quiet, enjoy-the-moment, well, moments.

"Hey, Leighton, hang back a minute. I couldn't help but be reminded of the first time you were over here, and it happened to be Christmas."

"I know I was thinking the same thing. It's crazy to think how much has changed since then, but also how much it's changed for the better. I couldn't be prouder of the work we've put in as a couple, and in life it's been awesome to grow with you," Leighton told me.

"I love you, sweets. I know today was probably just another reminder of that same bullshit your parents pulled on our first Christmas together. At least they were consistent. I know it doesn't make it any easier, but I think we've reached a point where you know where they stand and what to expect. I'm just a little concerned because as we have kids, your parents will become grandparents, but given how they act toward you, it'll be more like distant aunt and uncles."

"I know, right? That's what's been going through my head all day long when I found out. I shared in the moment with your mom, but never told mine. I didn't even want to tell her—

and not because I wasn't sure because it was early, but because I didn't want to get let down."

It pained me to watch Leighton go through this. It was probably part of the drive that pushed her to help so many people, to be so selfless and to give other people the support she felt she never had. She has given me an extra level of support that not everyone gets in their relationships. I understand that and try to work to ensure that in the off-season and when I'm home, I show her how important she is to me. It's not an easy life to travel as much as I do, and I know having kids will be hard to balance, but I think we're up for the challenge.

"I love you, Lei. I can only imagine the inner turmoil and conflict you must have been going through all day on our wedding day. Finding out you were pregnant and sharing it with my mom but feeling you shouldn't with yours. Though it probably feels more natural after all these years, you still have to feel guilty a bit. I'm sorry you're still in this situation."

"Thanks, Travis. It's a part of growing up the way I did. I just try and keep it in perspective.
When I look at many of those kids in New Orleans who are growing up without shoes, without medical care, or a ride to

school I realize I had it rough and definitely not the same as you, but they have it way worse off. Life is about perspective and when I look through their eyes, I grew up rich. It's like you said when I first came over to your house—you're roughing it here compared to the houses up the block."

"That's right, I did say that life is often just variations of perspective. One of the reasons I love you is the way you have taken what life has given you and turned it into a lifetime of giving back and improving the lives of countless others. Speaking of which, how's the clinic doing without you? I know you checked in a few times throughout the day. I wouldn't expect anything less."

"You know me too well. I called in a few times before the wedding, knowing that once the ceremony started it would be hard to find any time. It was the usual moving parts, vendors not doing their part, falling behind, and making it harder on the staff to administer medication to people who need it."

"Just like you, I'm staying on top of all the different moving parts even though you are states away. You are a driving force for that community and that clinic, I'm so proud of you, honey."

I remember that in the first couple of months of working at

the clinic, Leighton got tired of hearing from the staff that "It's just the way it is when you work at a clinic like that." She started getting involved more and more, stuck her nose in if you will, trying to find out what the issues were and why they weren't getting the items they needed. In typical Leighton fashion, if something was preventing her from doing her job, especially when caring for others, nothing was going to stop her. She went on an investigative journey, you might say. It took her about three weeks of countless calls and meetings with more people than I can remember before she found out that the biggest issue was funding.

It seemed that the person running the foundation just wasn't raising enough money, nor was she allocating the resources properly. Instead of getting upset, Leighton assumed that most people aren't malicious and this bunch was no exception. They just might need some help, she thought. So she reached out and offered to help them solve these issues through my professional basketball connections. Still, they had to clean up their office and books first. If she was going to get me involved and stick our necks out, she wanted to make sure everything was on the up-and- up and covered properly.

Not being one who was strong in accounting, she started

One Golden Day

taking classes in QuickBooks. She then helped the head of the charity get their hands around all the issues with funding, where the money was going, and what wasn't getting paid. It was just a matter of bills not getting paid properly; too much going to the wrong place. Leighton found it wasn't someone stealing or trying to hide money, but simply being in a little over their head. Once they got settled in, I realized where the shortcomings were and what exactly needed to be done. That's when Leighton asked me to get the Pelicans and their community outreach programs involved. This allowed her and the clinics to make a bigger impact since they had the tools, medications, and items needed to serve the communities fully.

After two years of being a strong driving force with the Pelicans in growing the clinics, she and the head of the Pelicans' outreach program came up with a great supplemental program to help underprivileged kids with schooling. They wanted to be a community center, not just a clinic—a place that felt like home, like a mom for the community. Leighton is one of the most amazing women in my life, and I've been surrounded by some pretty sweet ones.

Leighton interrupted my thoughts. "Travis, we should probably be getting in there to watch the movie. I wonder what

One Golden Day

your dad is putting on."

"From the looks of it, it's *Die Hard*, and they're arguing over whether or not it's a Christmas movie. This is amazing. I honestly can't think of a better way to wind down a day then by watching *Die Hard* on our wedding day, Mrs. Golden."

"Oooh, I like the sound of that. 'Mrs. Golden'."

"Side note, I don't see Father Dan in there. I bet he's upstairs smoking. I know he said he quit, but I doubt it. I'm going to see if I can catch him and have a chat."

"Okay, Travis, I'll be in there with the family." Leighton kissed me and smiled.

"See you in a few, Mrs. Golden." I loved saying that as much as she loved hearing it.

One Golden Day

18

Well At Least Our Wedding Will Be Memory Filled

As I made my way up the stairs through the back of the house, I could see a silhouette of a man matching Father Dan's build, with some smoke puffs coming up. As I walked out, he tried putting the cigarette away quickly, but it was too late; the damage was already done. I had caught him with a heater in his hand.

"Hey, Father Dan, what's up? Great night for a smoke I see."

"I was about to say, 'I don't know what you're saying,' but it's obvious you caught me."

"You could say I caught you with the smoking gun? I know that's a little corny, but oh well." "Please stop, that was brutal. That poor sense of humor reminds me of your dad. It's

One Golden Day

uncanny.

You look like him and your taste in comedy is just as poor."

He got me with that one. "Ouch, fair enough, that was well deserved. How's your night going? Are you enjoying the breezy Amarillo night?"

"Not just the nights, Travis. I haven't ever seen a sunset like this in my life. It's been a sight to see. Thank you for inviting me here."

"This is nothing. We should take you hiking tomorrow morning or in the early evening to see a sunrise or sunset from the Palo Duro Canyon. There is nothing quite like that, especially a sunset, because it just keeps going. If you're at the top watching it to the west, you can watch it for hours."

"I'll have to take you up on that before either of us leave. By the way, when do you and Leighton head back to New Orleans?"

"We'll be in town for a few more days. We don't leave until the end of the week. We're not doing a honeymoon quite yet, it's too close to the season, but we're okay with that. We'll do one in the off-season. I should have planned to propose to her at a better time."

"Speaking of that, how *did* you propose to her? You two

One Golden Day

dated for quite some time, even moved to New Orleans together for a few years before you got married." Father Dan sounded like my mom. "You sound like my parents right now. Leighton and I were happy, in love, and in no hurry to get married. It wasn't a choice; we just didn't force it. As for proposing, that was kind of poorly done, half-assed, and rushed. I had a grand plan, but it all fell apart during a storm in New Orleans."

My plan for the proposal had started off great. I had a grand plan to propose to Leighton when I got home from a long road trip out West with the Pelicans. I bought a ring when in Dallas, had my mom meet me there to help pick it out, and even stole one of Leighton's rings to ensure I got the right size. My mom picked it up a few days later and mailed it to the team facility so when I got back it would be waiting for me. Then I could pop the question to my girl with the perfect ring, in an amazing town.

All of that changed when we landed back in New Orleans on one of the bumpiest flights we'd had all season, which put us in an hour late. Leighton had been texting me like crazy all day, making sure we were okay. She was worried because there was a big storm brewing and about to hit the coast. That's probably the only thing I don't like about New Orleans. I don't

One Golden Day

mind the storms, but I do mind the damage they do, the travel they upset, and all the extra stuff that comes with them.

The rain and the wind aren't too bad, especially if you live in or near the French Quarter like we do. It was built on a natural levee, which means when the weather is crazy it holds up great. Water runs off and houses hold true, even if water levels rise. During Hurricane Katrina, the French Quarter was saved because of this historic concept of planning of building along a natural levee. I can get into more than that, telling you what I've learned about the storm and how the city was affected, but let's get back to this storm and my botched proposal.

Finally, our flight landed in New Orleans and I got in my car to drive back to the stadium to unpack and grab the ring. Leighton was a bit confused about why I wasn't coming straight home. I had to keep making excuses that she wasn't buying and she kept calling me as I was driving in the rain.

"Hey, Leighton, what's up? I'm just driving to the arena, then I'll be home in a bit."

"Why can't you come straight home? I'm worried about you in this storm. Can't it wait until tomorrow?" I couldn't tell her that I needed to pick up her wedding ring.

One Golden Day

"Leighton, coach, and the training staff said they want me back to do a quick treatment, especially with the way my back and hips have been. Then I can come home. They pay me a lot of money; I need to listen. I'll be home soon. It's just a thirty-minute treatment."

None of my treatments were that short and she wasn't going to buy this shit, but it was all I had at the moment. I tried to get her off the phone so I could focus on driving in this shit storm. But she wanted to talk, get me home, and make sure I was safe. I get it, but I just want to get that ring.

"Your treatments always take longer. Why is this one short?"

"We did some of it on the plane and we just need to finish at the arena. I'll be home as soon as I can, I promise."

"Something doesn't seem right, Mr. Travis Golden. You aren't lying to me, are you?"

"No, I am not, I wouldn't dare." Yes I was, and she can usually tell.

"You sure sound like you are."

"I'm just nervous talking to you in this rainstorm, trying to focus on the roads."

"I guess that's a good enough excuse for now. We'll see

One Golden Day

when you get home." She bought that. "I love you, Lei. I'll text you when I'm done and on my way home."

"Okay. Love you too. Be safe."

Finally at the arena and all through security, I got in to check in my stuff and unpack. Then I had to track down the equipment manager. They were in charge of all the mail that came to the facility. This ended up taking much longer than anticipated because they hadn't come in, so we had to try and call them. I should have just given up, went home, and tried again later, but now I was fixated on getting the ring, getting home, and proposing to Leighton. I knew she was beyond pissed at me. I had lied to her and felt the only way I wasn't sleeping on the couch or at the arena was with that ring in hand.

She was texting me, calling me, blowing me up, asking me what the delay was. At this point, I was already at an hour plus. And I was giving her excuses like the trainers were late to the facility from the weather, and we fell behind.

"Travis, just come home. You can get treatment tomorrow, or I can give you a massage tonight.

We can even do stim at home; we have the equipment."

"I'm here now. I might as well just wait it out and get it

taken care of, so I don't have to do it tomorrow. We have an off day tomorrow; I'd like to stay home." I hope we did; I hadn't even checked the schedule.

"I guess that seems fair. I just want you home safe with me, you've been gone for a week. You're basically home, but not home. GET YOUR ASS HOME, TRAVIS GOLDEN!!!"

"Understood, Ms. LEIGHTON!!!!"

Okay, so I think I bought myself a little bit of time but still no equipment manager, no one even here. Where is everyone, am I the only one dumb enough to come out here on a night like tonight? Come to think of it, no one is here? I mean no one—no coaches, no players, no staff.

Just me and a few security guards. Hey, maybe the head security could help me.

"Tony, what's up? Anyway, you can look for a piece of mail with my name on it? It would be in the equipment room. I spoke to the equipment manager yesterday to confirm he got it."

"You know I can't do that. Why the hell did you even drive here in this shit? The only reason we're here is in case they need to use it as a shelter and to ensure no one does anything stupid."

One Golden Day

"Come on, man. I shipped something super important, and I need to get it. It can't wait until tomorrow." I was acting like a junky looking for a fix.

"Damn Travis, you ship yourself some good Kush or some shit? If you share it with me, you got a deal," he said jokingly, giving me a hard time.

"You know I don't smoke. I'm one of the few in the NBA who doesn't. I shipped a ring for my girl here, and I want to propose to her today. It has to be today."

"Why today, and why did you ship it here, man? Not that bright. If you give me a good enough reason, I'll see what I can do."

"Today is a really important date for me. Leighton doesn't remember it I don't think, but it's the anniversary of the first time I met her. Not our first date, but when I first met her. It would be a huge deal to me. Come on, man, hook me up."

"Oh man, let me call the manager to see if he's cool with it."

Tony disappeared for a good twenty minutes, which felt like an even longer time because Leighton was texting me, asking for an ETA. I just stopped answering because I was tired of lying to her. Maybe she was getting mad because she'd done something nice. Maybe she did remember what that day was.

258

One Golden Day

"Okay, I just spoke to him. He said it's in the office in his top drawer with your name on it. I'll grab it for you. Next time try to plan a little bit better." He was being nice but salty at the same time.

"Come on, man, it's not like I get to choose the NBA schedule or our travel days. I'm doing the best I can."

"You could have ordered the ring a lot earlier, and planned better, Bro. Come on, you know that."

"Good point, thanks Tony. I owe you one, maybe some Kush, ha-ha," I said jokingly as I ran away.

"Just get out of here and be safe."

I sprinted through the area, ring in hand, jumped in my car, and started driving home. I then texted Leighton and said, "phone almost dead, charging in the car, OMW HOME!" All I got back was a heart and a smiley face. I might be able to salvage this after all. I just needed to get home in one piece. Luckily the drive from the arena to our place off Frenchman was a short one down the quarter. I just shot down Poydras over to Decatur and before I knew it I was pulling into our driveway.

As I walked up the steps to our place, I saw Leighton standing in the doorway waiting for me. She was blocking the

One Golden Day

entryway, which kept me in the rain just long enough for me to get drenched. Well played Lei, but you're going to feel a little bit differently when I get down on one knee.

"Are you going to let me in, Lei, or you going to keep me out here getting wet as punishment

for being late?" She was sitting there, smirking, thinking about it.

"I'm not sure. Do you know what day today is, Travis?" Yup, but I was going to play coy. "Hmm, well, it's Monday, and tomorrow is Tuesday. So..."

"Travis, you really don't know what today is?" She was getting a little red. "You mean other than the anniversary of the day that you threw up on me?"

"Get in here you asshole. If you knew what today was, what the hell were you doing taking so long getting your ass home? I cooked dinner and everything, and wanted it to be special, but you took two hours longer than you should have."

Just as she was getting pissed at me, she started walking away. She made her way over to the kitchen, telling me how the food was cold, that everything was ruined, and how she didn't know how I could be so selfish on such an important day, *especially* if I knew what day it was. At this point she was rambling on. She hadn't even noticed that I'd set my stuff down, knelt down on one knee, and was waiting for her to turn around. I was there a good three to four minutes, which felt like an eternity. Eventually, I started laughing a little bit, that's what got her to turn around.

"What the hell is so ..." "Leighton, will you marry me?"

"Son of bitch, Travis Golden, this is why you were late, I HATE YOU!" "Is that a yes or a no?"

"Yes, it's a yes, of course, it's a yes. I love you so much, Travis Golden."

I know it wasn't the most romantic way to propose, but it fit Leighton and me—it fit our lives, our story, and our relationship perfectly. We were that kind of people—the ones who are

comfortable getting married in the city, in someone's backyard, by our friend, or in Vegas. We have been through so much, and had experienced so much of life together. We were just happy being together. The rest was secondary.

Father Dan was incredulous. "Let me get this straight. You kept your now wife waiting half the day while you tried tracking down the ring on an anniversary that both of you knew about—and all this in the middle of a brutal storm? She kept blowing up your phone, not buying your shit story; eventually, you got home and proposed to her. Does that sum it up?"

"Pretty much. And it sounds pretty rough, I know, but that's how Leighton and I function; it's in a different space."

"If we're going to stay out here mind if I smoke another cigarette? When I have a few drinks, I really enjoy a few heaters."

"I could see that. I worked in bars for a long time. Usually the smoke breaks picked up as the night went on. The more people drank, the more they smoked. I'm assuming it's the mix of nicotine stimulant and alcohol depressant."

"No one asked for science, but I could see that."

Father Dan fought back a few coughs; they sounded pretty deep if you ask me, even for someone who had been smoking and drinking as much as he had. He might be a man of the cloth, still, he has devoted his life to others for almost five decades. That stress, from a lifetime of enjoying a few cigarettes and a drink or two, adds up. I had noticed him coughing a few times earlier, but this cough seemed to be deep; it didn't sound good.

"Father Dan, that cough is pretty rough. When's the last

time you got that checked out?"

"It's nothing. I've been dealing with this on and off for a while."

"If you say so, but you should get that looked into. I mean Leighton at least should give you the once-over. I'm going to go grab her."

I went inside to get Leighton but before I could get a few feet from Father Dan, I heard a thud—a very distinctive sound like when someone passes out and doesn't catch themselves. I looked outside to see Father Dan on the ground, and I screamed downstairs.

"Leighton, get up here ASAP!! Father Dan passed out, HEY!" "What!!??, I'm on my way." Leighton sprinted up the stairs. "Call 911! I'll get to work on Father Dan and check on him."

This was one crazy night, to say the least. I called 911, gave them all the pertinent information, then began working with Leighton, helping her in any way I could. She was able to get Father Dan up a bit. He was breathing in a shallow way and he was barely conscious.

"Leighton, any idea what it is? He was coughing really bad. His cough and lungs sounded so deep. It almost sounded like

One Golden Day

when I had that brutal bronchitis in college a few years ago."

"With his age, his smoking, and drinking it could be a ton of different things. That's why I had you call 911. They need to check him out, get him to a hospital, and do a full workup. You can see the petechial hemorrhage on his skin; he definitely had some oxygen loss, that's the biggest issue."

Before I could get any other word out, I heard my mom guiding the EMTs through the house to the back where we were with Father Dan. They got to work quickly and started going through their checklist. Watching them, my wife talked back and forth about Father Dan's vitals, what she had been able to ascertain, and what she had done to help. A lot of information was communicated in a short period of time.

As they began to load up Father Dan, you could see him starting to move a little bit, but he didn't seem good. It almost seemed as though he was struggling, fighting for air, convulsing, and looking worse than when he'd passed out. Leighton rode with him in the ambulance, while I grabbed Mom and Dad and we piled in the car and headed over the hospital, leaving Chris and Terra behind. With her being almost six months pregnant and having traveled halfway across the globe, she needed to get some rest. She and Chris decided to stay back, clean up the house, and relax a bit. We would keep them informed, not to mention they needed some alone time to talk about everything that had happened that day.

"I hope he's going to be okay, Mom. His cough sounded really bad. I told Leighton it sounded deeper and worse than when I was fighting that case of bronchitis in college. Remember the one that kept me out of school for almost two weeks?"

"You were pretty sick back then, but you were also young and able to overcome it. Father Dan has led a different life. He's been to parts of the world with different bacteria and viruses. I just hope he's okay. Honey, do you have any idea what might be going on?" Mom looked more worried than normal.

"I know he's been dealing with some health issues the past couple years, but he hasn't been forthcoming as to what they were. I've been trying to get more info out of him since he's been here, but he's great at changing the subject. The only hope is to see what the doctors say when he

gets admitted to the hospital. We might also get some more info from Leighton."

The drive to the hospital was short, but it felt long, it felt like an eternity—almost as if we had hit every single red

One Golden Day

light along the way. At each red light, you could hear the three of us slow down our breathing and almost hear the gears in our heads turning. We were trying to not show our fear. But it's hard to not show concern late at night, after experiencing a day like that day had been, ending with a trip to the emergency room.

One Golden Day

19

Seems Fitting to End the Day Here

When we finally made it to the hospital and found a place to park, the walk in felt different. We huddled up close and linked hands, which for a moment, brought me back to when I was a kid. Specifically, I was referring to those times when your parents made you hold their hand for safety because you were in a parking lot. There was no reason to do it, we all just instinctively did it, probably to feel close and protected.

As we entered the emergency room we saw Leighton sitting in the waiting room. She waved us over with a troubled look on her face. Things didn't look good if I was judging by her expression. I had thought perhaps Father Dan had passed away in the ambulance on the way over to the hospital, but if that had happened, I would have hoped she would have called us right away.

"Leighton, is everything okay? You look beyond worried." My dad stepped up while Mom and I were still looking for words.

"No, it's not. Father Dan is struggling to breathe. He's struggling badly; he has pretty bad lung failure. I'd be surprised if he makes it through the night. Even if they stabilize him, I'm not sure how much damage has already been done from the loss of oxygen."

"It was that bad on the ride over here? They weren't able to improve it?" I was so lost.

"He was struggling so badly that they had to use the machine to breathe for him just to get some oxygen into his system."

After the back-and-forth for a good twenty minutes with Leighton, it was clear to see that Father Dan was in for a fight, one he might lose. He had lived an amazing life, done so much good work, and had had a lasting impact on the lives of so many, me included. I remember working in a soup kitchen with him when I was in high school. I spent the afternoons

One Golden Day

helping to organize and move donations to their storage facility. I then organized everything by expiration date to ensure the stuff that needed to be used first didn't end up being wasted.

You may or may not be surprised at how many people pack up their cupboards when moving or when a loved one dies but don't look at the dates on anything. Then they give us three boxes of food to feel great about themselves, but we might be able to use only twenty percent of it. I remember a lady once brought in four boxes of food. All of it was well past the expiration dates. She got mad at us because we wouldn't take it. Father Dan's exchange with her made me laugh then and still makes me smile. She kept insisting we give it to the poor people who were hungry. This, despite the fact that it had expired. He said if she was willing to eat a can of expired peaches with him on the spot he'd take the boxes. If not, she'd have to take the boxes back. As expected, she lost her shit.

We spent most of the next three hours going back and forth, sharing our favorite Father Dan stories and laughing and crying a bit. It felt like a funeral because on some level we knew what was really going on, and what we were going to have to go through at some point. It was just a matter of time. The four of us were quite calm, accepting what lay ahead. Of any of us, my

One Golden Day

father had the deepest relationship with Father Dan. They went back to childhood, having been classmates in grade school and continuing on all the way through high school. Their parents were friends who had vacationed together a few times.

Dad told a story of the two boys getting together one summer when they were teenagers, breaking into a community pool in the middle of the night to impress a couple of girls. That didn't go over so well with the local police who caught them. The girls took off, leaving Dad and Father Dan high and dry with the cops, who ended up calling their parents in the middle of the night. Luckily it was back in the day, and my dad and Father Dan—just *Dan* back then—hadn't gotten into any real trouble, so the cops let them go.

Before Dad could continue with another story of the two young men getting into trouble, a doctor walked into the room. "Is there anyone out here for Father Dan Havron?" he asked everyone in the room. "I know someone came with him in the ambulance, but no one got her name."

"That would be me, I came with him, but his closest thing to family is over here," Leighton replied.

"Hi, my name is Mr. Golden. Father Dan doesn't have any remaining relatives. He was an only child and when his parents

One Golden Day

passed, he was all that was left. What can I do for you?"

"We have a bit of a problem that we need some help with." The doctor looked a bit disheveled.

"What can I do for you? Is he okay? I'm assuming he can't talk and that's what you need me for." Dad was right on.

"Correct, he also had a DNR, which we eventually found when doing his paperwork. But this was after we revived him and got him on a respirator."

"What can I do for you then? If he has a DNR, what do you need from me?"

The doctor and my father spent the next ten or so minutes talking about how they needed someone not related to the hospital to pull the plug. Since they'd already made one mistake, they were looking for someone else to fix the problem is what it sounds like.

"Let me talk it over with my family for a bit, give them a little bit of time to think it over. You're not asking me to actually do it, simply sign the form, I'm assuming?" My dad looked concerned.

"Correct, sir. It's a procedural item, we would need to take him off the respirator. I'll give you all the time you need, just ask one of the nurses to page me and I'll come back down. In the meantime if you want to see him, he's in stable condition. You can go back to his room."

My dad came over, whispered into my mom's ear, and took her back into the heart of the hospital to see Father Dan. They were gone for a good forty-five minutes. I can only imagine what they were talking about back there, what they had to deal with. In my usual inpatient manner, I was up walking around, pacing the waiting room, while Leighton was sitting there calmly.

"Travis, are you ever going to sit down, or is this just how you're going to be?"

"Lei, you know the answer to that. I'm going to keep pacing around. We just got married, and the man who did our wedding is in the hospital on life support, and my father might have to pull the plug on his best friend, so to speak. It's a bit stressful."

"I get it, Travis, but when you're on the basketball court, you don't get frantic just because things get a little hectic or stressful. You stay calm and collected. I'm just asking you to tap into that same approach."

"The difference is I put in a ton of work that makes me feel prepared and in control in those moments. I can't put work into feeling control in a situation that involves the death of a close friend of my dad's."

I knew Leighton was just trying to calm me down because when my parents finally did come back out, I was going to have to be focused and relaxed. The last thing my dad needed was me going a mile a minute crazy, riling him up and making him feel worse. Leighton did have a good point, but I made a good point in reverse too. High-stress environments that I have worked in, or feel prepared in, seem easy; I can stay calm. Counter to that, though, I will get anxious in environments I have little to no experience in, such as this. It had been a whirlwind since I'd seen

Father Dan fall to the ground, and I hadn't allowed myself to process it.

"Your dad should be out soon; you need to be calm by the time he gets here, especially for him. To support him. You know that. I'm just trying to help."

"Okay. I'll sit down, try to slow down my breathing, and practice some of the relaxing techniques we do in yoga."

"Perfect. That's a great idea, Travis."

Leighton was trying to coax me down like a puppy that had run away. All she needed to add was the *old, good boy*, and it would have been complete. After she talked me down, got me to focus on my breathing, and slowed me down, I saw that my dad had made his way out of the hospital area and into the waiting room. He had a horrific look on his face, and eyes so puffy he looked like he had gone on a bender for a week.

"Dad, are you okay? What happened back there; how bad did he look?"

"He didn't look good at all. I reached out to the parish where he was staying and spoke to one of Father Dan's superiors for a little bit. We both agreed the proper thing to do was to sign the paperwork and have him taken off the ventilator. It was the hardest thing I think I've ever had to do."

I leaned in and gave my dad a huge hug. "Dad, I love you. Anything I can do just let me know. Do you want to stay around a little longer, or do you want to get out of here and head home?"

"I'd like to get out of here, and preferably stop and grab something to drink first. I need to take the edge off before I go home and have to pack up all his stuff."

As we started walking to the store, I texted Terra and Chris, explaining to them what had happened. I also asked them to clean up the spare bedroom where Father Dan had been

One Golden Day

staying and pack it all up for Dad. I told them that it was going to be hard for him to do that, and the quicker we cleaned it up, the better. He could go through it and deal with it at his own pace that way, without having to look at it that night. Chris texted back quickly, saying Terra was already asleep in her room, but he would take care of it.

As we'd finished texting, I tried to think of a place to take Dad.

"Dad, do you have any place in particular, you want to go? Or just anywhere at this point?" "Your choice. Just get me a stiff drink and decent atmosphere so I can relax." He looked drained.

"Dad, if your biggest concern is just dealing with Father Dan's stuff, it's already taken care of. Why don't we go home, relax with a drink on the couch, talk and reminisce, and then crash. It's been a long day."

"Travis, did you message Terra and Chris already?"

"Yeah, I asked them to clean up his stuff for you, so you wouldn't have to. I'd rather you be mad at me then stressed about that."

"Thanks, kiddo, yeah. Let's just go home then and have a drink on the couch."

One Golden Day

The rest of the ride home we all sat in silence, thinking about how the events of the day had gone from one end of the spectrum to the other: Taking a turn from joy to sadness, delaying the wedding so that my father could make it on time, Leighton finding out she was pregnant, and me going out back during the extra delay to shoot hoops. Also, it had turned out that Mom hadn't run home to get me a basketball, but to get a pregnancy test for Leighton and she'd used the ball as an excuse. At the reception, we'd watched Leighton's parents remind her why they were merely the people she was born to, not the people that loved and supported her. We watched Terra show up with the baby in her womb, found out it was Chris's baby, and learned he was probably moving to France now.

After all of that, after all of the craziness that we'd gone through—the ups and downs, the crying, the fighting, and the shock—ending the night with Father Dan's passing seemed so impossible, even when I'd seen Father Dan fall to the ground. Hearing that sound will forever live in my memory. I didn't think his life would end as it had.

"Hey Dad, you said Father Dan had some other health issues. I know we're almost home, and I'll leave it once we pull in, but what were they? After talking to Leighton and seeing

One Golden Day

how he reacted, something had to be there."

"He had been fighting lung cancer for a few years and had decided to let it run its course. He didn't want treatment. He was okay with handling it that way, but I kept pushing him to do something to at least deal with the pain. This was my biggest concern, him going out like this. I always thought it would end with him in some third world country doing work, not in our backyard."

"I love you, Dad. I know Father Dan was a close friend of yours, I'm sorry it ended like this too."

"I'm sorry for you guys. This is your wedding day, and it's been one for the ages. You found out your sister is carrying your best friend's baby, the priest officiating at your wedding died, and your in-laws acted like assholes after their daughter, the bride, had to save the life of one of them. Sorry Leighton, but they did."

"You're fine, Mr. Golden, trust me. I know they're assholes. But I'd say tonight was Golden."

"Yeah, I agree with Leighton. Just plain old Golden!"

For more updates sign up at

www.BHPubs.com

The Neil Baggio Universe

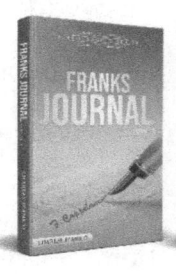

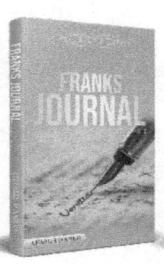